TEXAS TRAMP

"You damn good for white man," Wantabe said.

"Thanks. Now, can we talk about Penny, the yellow hair?"

Wantabe shook his head. "Tomorrow, after next contest. Rest well, white man Spur. Tomorrow is the last contest, the fight of the knife and rawhide."

Spur looked puzzled for a moment, unsure of what the Comanche was talking about; then he remembered. It was a knife fight in which both men held one end of a three foot long piece of rawhide by their teeth. To drop the end of the rawhide was to forfeit the fight and your life. It was a battle to the death! And if Spur didn't win, Penny would lose any hope of ever being saved.

SPUR #40

TEXAS TRAMP

DIRK FLETCHER

LEISURE BOOKS NEW YORK CITY

A LEISURE BOOK®

September 2006

Published by

Dorchester Publishing Co., Inc.
200 Madison Avenue
New York, NY 10016

ISBN 0-8439-3523-5

The name "Leisure Books" and the stylized "L" with design are trademarks of Dorchester Publishing Co., Inc.

Printed in the United States of America.

Visit us on the web at www.dorchesterpub.com.

TEXAS TRAMP

Chapter One

Fifteen Comanche warriors rode out of the sun, slashing into the large Texas ranch, screeching their war cries, firing rifles and driving two cowboys to the cover of the bunkhouse.

The attackers did not have a carefully thought-out plan. They simply charged in and attacked the wooden pen where the horses were, opening the gate and driving 40 mounts out. Then half the warriors herded the animals to the west and north.

Two warriors rode to the barn and threw live coals onto the hay. Within minutes it was a raging mountain of flames.

Penny Wallington huddled in the outhouse 40 yards from the ranch house. She heard the Indians attack and couldn't believe it. They'd had no Indian trouble in months. When the barn exploded in flames, she huddled lower in the small structure, hoping the Indians would ignore it.

She looked up in alarm as something rattled the

door, which was locked inside with a hook and eye. A moment later the small structure tipped, then crashed over to the side, ripping away from the floor. She fell with the wall and rolled into the open.

A large Comanche warrior leaned down from his war pony, scooped her up, tossed her across his mount and galloped hard past the burning barn to the northwest.

Penny was too surprised and furious to scream. She bounced along, blood rushing to her head, feeling like a rag doll on a runaway horse.

She remembered hearing a few rifle shots behind her and some yelling; then as it all faded, she knew she was about to faint. She did.

Penny had no way of knowing how long she lay there unconscious, but when she came back to reality, the Indian pony still trotted across the flatness of the Texas range. She looked around and realized that there were a dozen or more Indians driving a herd of horses, mostly Bar-W mounts.

Penny screeched and grabbed the savage's foot. When he snorted and kicked her on the shoulder, she let go of his foot, but kept bellowing in anger and frustration.

When the jolting stopped, Penny realized that the horse had halted. She turned and tried to look up at her captor, who caught her by the waist and lifted her upward until her head was over the horse's back. When he lowered her again she was astride the beast. It took Penny several minutes for her head to clear and her eyes to get used to riding upright again. She took in the situation quickly, having been born and bred on a ranch.

Yes, 12 to 15 Comanche raiders. They had hit the ranch fast and hard, driven off all the mounts in the corral and now charged northwest toward their camp or hideout. She estimated they had stolen about 50 horses.

The ranch would send out a force to recover the mounts, and she wondered if anyone saw her being captured. She doubted it. They were too busy defending the ranch house and trying to stop the theft of the horses.

No! Someone must have seen her. They finally would find her missing and mount a rescue. They had to.

Penny wore an everyday calico dress, so practical on the ranch. It wasn't what she'd wear when she was with her father in Washington, D.C., where he was a United States senator. But she had been home to see the birth of a new foal from her favorite mare. The little creature had been born a week ago and now was so frisky he was a delight. She had planned on going back to Washington at the end of the month.

With great care, Penny turned to look at her captor. She could tell he was large for an Indian. He had his arms around her, holding her in place and also holding the hackamore that helped guide his war pony.

She saw a lean, rugged face, with a strong nose and deep-set dark eyes. His skin was not red at all but slightly brown, as if he had a good suntan. His chin was square, and he had three red slashes of paint on each cheek. He wore a single eagle's feather in his black hair, which was long and braided in back.

He caught her looking at him and scowled.

"You are woman, you are mine. Be my third wife." The words came in the Comanche tongue, and though Penny couldn't understand him, she didn't like the tone of his voice.

For a moment dozens of stories and tales of white women captured by Indians came flooding back to

7

her. Tears leaped to her eyes and rolled down her cheeks.

"I'm tired and sore. Can't we stop and rest?" she asked, looking up at him over her shoulder.

He grunted, and to her it was obvious that he understood no more of her language than she did of his.

Penny tried to look behind but could find no sign of pursuit. The Indian laughed and said something she didn't understand.

The pace of the flight had slowed. The horses were being walked now, and the Comanche were keeping the animals closely grouped. They were excellent horsemen, as Penny had been told for years. Now she felt more than saw the way the warrior behind her controlled the animal they both rode. The Comanche seldom used the hackamore. Most of the directions to the animal came from the Indian's knees, legs and feet.

A slight pressure with a knee turned the horse one way or the other. Penny was amazed by the great horsemanship of the savages even as she shivered with fear. The reality of her plight soon settled over her. She had been too shocked to cry before, but now as the stories of white women as Indian slaves came back to her, she let the tears come. She cried, wiped tears from her eyes and cried again.

The warrior behind her snarled something, waited a moment, then hit her shoulder with his fist. He barked another command as she gasped at the pain.

The raid on the ranch had come almost at sunset, probably an hour before. She noticed how the warriors had ridden out of the setting sun, making them almost impossible to see until they were right on top of her. She had peered through cracks in the outhouse for a moment before huddling on the floor.

Now the sun had set, but they kept riding. Penny wondered how long she could stand this before she went crazy. At least she was sitting up now. Her head still ached from all of the jolting and swaying with her head and arms hanging downward. This was better.

They came to a small stream and let the horses drink. Though Penny had ridden the ranch most of her life, she couldn't remember this stream, having never ridden up this way much.

She asked to have a drink. The warrior didn't understand her, but he rode upstream from where the horses drank, slid off the mount and pulled her down. She slipped and fell to the ground. The warrior chuckled and fingered her long blonde hair which she had planned to wash and braid that night. Now she certainly wouldn't be doing that.

He pushed her toward the water, and she walked carefully. At least she had on sturdy shoes. At the stream, she knelt and lifted handfuls of water to drink.

The warrior watched her, snorted, bent his face into the clear water and drank his fill. He lifted up, settled back on his haunches and watched her.

He asked her something. Penny shook her head. "I don't understand you," she said.

He grunted, said a word and touched his bare chest. She frowned, and he did the same thing again.

"Wantabe," he said, and she nodded.

"Wantabe," she said and pointed to him. Then she pointed to herself. "Penny," she said.

He snorted and laughed, pointed to her and said a word that did not sound at all like her name. He said it again, and she listened closely.

"Penuu," he said and pointed to her. She shrugged,

9

nodded, repeated his version of her name and pointed to herself.

Then he stood, caught her shoulder and pulled her to his horse. He lifted her up first and laughed when her full skirt settled down over his head. He brushed it aside, mounted behind her and slid both arms around her. His hands closed around both her breasts, and he grunted in evident satisfaction. He fondled them a moment, then released them and kicked the horse into motion.

The Indians had the animals moving again, and their course kept true to the northwest. Penny knew little of what lay far to the northwest except the Staked Plains, that vast plateau of desert where almost nothing grew and where it never rained. There was no source of water for hundreds of miles, or so she had been told. Surely they weren't going there.

An hour after their water stop, they heard a long wailing shout from ahead and soon came upon a large band of Indians and an even larger herd of horses and mules.

Even in the darkness, Penny could tell there were hundreds of horses, perhaps over 200. It must have been a fine raid for the Comanches.

They stopped with the main body and herded their horses into the larger group. Then the warriors scattered to small cooking fires where food was ready for them.

Wantabe cuffed Penny on the side of the head, grunted at her and motioned to the front. He called her Penuu, and she moved where he pointed.

It was a raider's camp—no tepees, only a few women to cook. Everything was packed onto horses for a sudden departure. They walked to a small cooking fire where Wantabe pushed Penny down to the ground, then squatted nearby.

The land had been as flat as an ironing board, but now it slanted and rolled a little. Penny wondered how far they had come and how anyone would ever find her. One woman cooked some kind of stew over the fire, and Penny didn't want to think what the meat in it might be.

By that time it was fully dark, and the night sounds came. A lonesome sounding bird wailed far off on the prairie. An owl hooted closer by. Crickets began their nightly romantic chirping.

Penny looked at Wantabe and motioned into the darkness. "The outhouse. I need to go to the outhouse," she said, knowing it sounded stupid, but she couldn't figure out how else to communicate with the savage.

He stared at her, unblinking, face passive, not responding in any way.

"Oh, damn you," she spat at him. Wantabe grinned. She got to her feet, then squatted and motioned to the blackness away from the fire.

This time Wantabe nodded. He stood, took her by the shoulder and led her away from the camp.

"Wait a minute. If you think I'm going to perform with you watching me . . ." She knew he couldn't understand her, but by that time her bladder was at the point of bursting. She squatted, pulled down her short bloomers, lifted her skirts and urinated.

Wantabe chuckled.

Back at the fire he pushed her down again, and the Indian woman handed her a bowl made from a hardy gourd. Inside was a soupy stew. Penny tried not to taste it. She fished out a piece of meat with her fingers and ate it, then tipped the bowl, drank the soup and chewed on anything else she found. She recognized some wild onions they must have found near a stream somewhere.

West Texas was not an easy place to live off the

land, unless you could stand a steady diet of lizards and rattlesnake steaks.

There was no water where they camped. Penny yearned to wash her face and arms, to strip to the waist and give herself a good bath, but that was impossible. She found Wantabe staring at her.

The night would mean sleeping. Would he attack her? Would he rape her right out here in the open?

Penny shivered. She was 18 and had been fondled once by a boy at a church picnic, but she'd never come any closer to a sexual experience than that. She watched Wantabe, but he made no move toward her.

A minute later she stretched out, turned on her stomach to protect herself and tried to sleep. A moment later she sensed him over her.

"No!" she shouted.

Wantabe laughed softly. He had a short piece of braided rawhide rope. He tied one end to her wrist, and the other end he held in his hand. If she moved an inch, he would know it.

Penny realized that she couldn't roll over. She would have to be on her stomach all night. She sighed. It was probably safer that way. She tried to sleep but couldn't.

When she felt the Comanche warrior run his hand through her hair, she breathed deeply as if she were sleeping. His hand went down her back to her bottom, then wedged between her legs. For a moment she wanted to scream. Then his hand withdrew, he gave a long sigh, and a moment later she heard him snoring softly.

Penny awoke at dawn with the sound of the camp breaking. There was no food. They got up, got on their mounts and rode away. This time Wantabe provided her with a small painted pony, one she was sure she had seen on the ranch. There was neither saddle nor blanket.

Already she was stiff and sore from yesterday's bareback ride. The sides of her inner thighs were rubbed red by the movement of the animal, and she screeched in pain as Wantabe lifted her onto the mount.

The screech died in her throat as he frowned at her. She tucked her long skirt under her bottom for a cushion and pulled the rest of her skirt so it protected her thighs from the rough hair of the pony.

Once they left the small wash where they had camped, she was surprised by the size of the party. She figured there must be at least 40 warriors and six or eight women, and they were driving at least 200 horses. These warriors would be considered extremely rich when they got back to their camp.

Where was the camp? She had heard of the Staked Plains, far to the northwest of their ranch, but she'd never been there. The cattlemen saw no reason to go up there at all, since it was too damn dry to support even one cow on 200 acres.

Before noon she sensed the excitement in the Comanches. They must be near their summer camp. They dropped into a small valley with a ribbon of water in the bottom and worked up it for five miles. Then she saw the camp.

The riverbanks were covered with tepees. Wantabe caught the hackamore of her pinto and led her horse straight to one of the larger tepees.

Women and children ran around, shouting and calling. Dogs barked. She caught the glorious smell of freshly roasted meat—venison or antelope she guessed.

Wantabe pulled her off the pony and pushed her forward. Two Indian women watched her. One was older, the other young and well into a pregnancy. He pushed Penny into the tepee, and for a moment she could see nothing.

Then Wantabe caught her and forced her down on a pallet of furs. His hands found her breasts, and he rubbed them so hard she whimpered. He pulled at her dress and motioned to her. She nodded. If he tore it she'd have nothing to wear. She undid the buttons and fasteners and pulled off the dress, then the petticoats. She sat there on the skins and furs, bare from her stomach down. Only a thin chemise covered her breasts. She folded her arms over her chest and glared at him.

Wantabe growled. He caught the chemise and ripped it off her. Then his hands held her breasts, and he laughed softly and rolled on top of her.

For a moment, Penny thought she was going to die. A minute later she was afraid that she wouldn't.

Chapter Two

Secret Service Agent Spur McCoy received the telegram in New Orleans, where he had just finished cleaning up a nasty counterfeiting case involving a million dollars worth of bogus United States bonds.

He said a hasty good-bye to a dark-eyed Creole girl and caught the first train north. He worked west until he at last reached Austin, Texas. From there it was a stagecoach rumble out to the small town of Sweet Springs. The sign at the edge of town boasted 456 residents and an elevation of 3,467 feet.

He slapped the dust off his corduroy jacket, reset his flat-crowned black Stetson with the row of Mexican silver pesos around it, and eased up to the boardwalk in front of the depot.

The thin man riding shotgun on the run tossed Spur's carpetbag to him and pointed down the street.

15

"Only two hotels in town. Best one is the Panhandle Palace. Ain't much of a palace, but it's the best we got."

Spur thanked him and headed in that direction. Nobody in town knew he was coming. He always liked it that way until he could get a sense of what was going on. This job seemed fairly simple. The resident United States senator from the great state of Texas had lost a daughter in a Comanche raid. He wanted her back.

Spur evaluated the town as he walked. It was in the middle of the high flat country of western Texas that some were calling the panhandle. It was about halfway up on the west side of the handle and not too far from the Staked Plains where almost nothing lived, not even grass.

Spur McCoy was the Secret Service agent responsible for most of the area west of the Mississippi River. He'd joined the agency when it first began in 1859 and was sent west because he could ride and shoot better than any of the other agents.

He worked mostly on orders sent him by wire from the headquarters at 61 Pennsylvania Avenue. William Wood was the director who had been appointed by President Lincoln and reappointed by each new President to date.

Agent McCoy stood six-feet two-inches tall and weighed a heavily muscled 185. He was as lithe and supple as a cougar stalking a five-point buck deer, kept himself in top condition and usually was tanned and fit from so much time outdoors. He was an expert with revolver, rifle, knife and whip and had more than once used his hands and feet as lethal weapons. His black hair was neatly trimmed but a little long in back, and he was clean shaven. He stared at the world from green eyes.

Spur grew up in New York City, where his

father had been a merchant. He had graduated from Harvard University and had served time in the Army of the Republic, attaining the rank of captain.

As he walked down the street he remembered that Sweet Springs gained its name from a set of clear water springs at the edge of town below a small outcropping. One of the locals had told Spur about it as they rode past in the coach. That was why people stopped here originally. Then a store went up, and soon there was a semblance of a settlement.

When the cattlemen moved in, the town grew further, developing stores to meet the needs. The first was the general store, then came a saddle and leather goods shop to provide saddles and harnesses for the ranches.

By now there were more than 30 different retail and service stores in town, including one for shoe and boot repair.

Spur checked in at the Panhandle Palace, got a room on the second floor front, 212, and washed up using a large ceramic bowl and water pitcher.

Ten minutes later he found the Morgan County sheriff's office and stepped inside. Spur guessed it would be a three-man office, consisting of the sheriff and two deputies. He saw a young man wearing a silver star at the counter that extended across the width of the building. Slightly to the rear sat a man with his back to Spur, showing a crown of silver hair.

The kid looked up.

"Is the sheriff in?" Spur asked.

The young man turned and looked at the older man.

"Yep, I be here. Just a cotton-picking minute."

Spur grinned, recognizing the words and the voice.

17

"Hell, I was hoping this county had a real he-man sheriff, not some tin-badge-toting Eastern dude who don't know his elbow from a horse thief."

The silver-haired man stiffened for a moment, then chuckled. He spoke without turning.

"Zeb, tell that ornery, flea-toting maverick of a jackass that I don't hold no court with no damned federal agents." The older man turned, a wide grin on his face.

"Been a long time, Ben," Spur said, holding his hand over the counter.

"Hell of a long time, Spur McCoy. You still eating at the public trough for Washington?"

"Yeah, they can't get rid of me. General Halleck tries to get me killed off out here in the Wild West, but it just ain't happened yet."

Spur had been shocked right down to his boot toes when Ben Johnson had turned around. The man looked 70. His rugged face had sagged, his sharp blue eyes were watery and pale, his firm jaw had slacked, and he hadn't shaved for three or four days, leaving a wispy stubble rather than a beard.

He moved slowly to the counter and took Spur's hand. His big mitt came forward gradually, and there was no grip at all in the fingers. Spur tried to cover up his surprise, anger, then sense of loss. Ben Johnson had been one of Texas's best lawmen, with a reputation far and wide for running clean towns, cleaning up dirty ones, and keeping whole counties in line. He wasn't even a shadow of his former domineering presence.

The watery eyes looked up.

"You in town on business?"

"Yep. The senator's daughter."

"Damned shame. Come into my office and sit a spell."

Spur moved around the counter and sat in a chair beside the old man's desk.

The sheriff looked up and blinked quickly to control his emotion. "Penny's only eighteen, a real beauty. Doesn't spend a lot of time at the ranch but came home from Washington to help her favorite mare come to foal. Due to go back a few days after she was grabbed."

"Comanches?"

"Way we figure. Some northern band on a long raid. Some of them have been going all the way into Mexico to steal horses. That's their job—stealing horses and trading them for what they need. Trade a lot with other Indian groups."

"When did this happen?"

"A week ago yesterday. Eight days that poor darling has been in the clutches of the Comanches."

"Any way of knowing what band of Comanches grabbed her?"

"None. The ranch sent out six men to track the horses. Kinda of hard to hide fifty head. They soon came to what they figured was tracks of a herd of more than two hundred moving northwest. After a day and a half of tracking, they lost them in a swampy river area."

"Lost them or got scared they were too close to the savages?"

The old lawman grunted, lifted one foot and massaged it. He slipped off his shoe and worked on the foot through a brown stocking with both hands.

"Little rheumatiz creeping up on me," he said. "I figure the cowhands decided nothing was worth getting scalped that far from home. No way they could have handled a whole Comanche band, so they turned back."

The lawman put his foot down and then, in what

Spur figured was an unconscious move, rubbed his right hand with his left one. He flexed the fingers slowly, but none of them would go out straight. He glanced up at Spur and sighed.

"Yeah, you're right, Spur. I'm falling apart. Seems like damn near nothing works right anymore. I don't dare get on a horse. Do my traveling by buggy. Don't think I've fired my six-gun in over a year. Just can't draw anymore. Damn hand won't work right. Too old to learn with my left, but then it ain't one hell of a lot better."

"Any young bloods around looking to make a rep?"

Ben stared at Spur a moment and nodded. "Hell, always was, always will be. One came in here last week. Zeb there took care of him. He was tough and young and brash and wanted to meet me just to shake my hand. Zeb said he had a brand-new leather tied hard against his thigh and a polished hogleg showing. His hand twitched over the butt of it like he couldn't wait to call me out."

"Don't wear a gun, Ben; then nobody can draw on you."

"Seen it happen the other way, ten years ago, to Phil Watson. Don't think you knew him. Damn fine lawman. His hand went bad on him so he never packed a piece. One day a snot-nosed kid drew down on him in an alley and killed him. Got away clean. His version of the story was the one everyone talked about. How he beat Phil to the draw on Main Street in Abilene in broad daylight."

Spur shook his head. "It's a damn bad situation. First I got to see what's what about this senator's girl; then we'll talk and figure out something. I hear Chicago is nice this time of the year."

"Snows too damn much up there."

"True. We'll figure something. How do I find the senator's spread, the Bar-W?"

Spur took directions, rented a horse at the livery, picked up a Spencer rifle seven shot in the .52-caliber size and pocketed a box of ammo and three spare ammo tubes.

The Bar-W was easy to find. The near edge of the range began less than a mile north of town and stretched more than 20 miles to the northwest. The Sweet Springs River headed toward the spread and provided most of the water used by the Bar-W.

Less than five miles out of town the Sweet Springs River made a big bend and sired a copse of cottonwoods and juniper. The ranch house was a three-story affair made of lumber. More than a dozen barns, sheds and other buildings made the place look like a small town.

The lane leading to the spread had a gate made of 15-foot-high beams upward and across the top, with a large Bar-W brand cut deep into a slab of glued wood that was six feet square.

He rode through the gate and toward the buildings a quarter of a mile ahead. He wasn't challenged. By the time he got to the first barn, a hand ambled out and waved. He had a six-gun in leather.

"Afternoon. Looking for the Bar-W?"

"Right, this must be it. I'm supposed to talk with a man named Loren Cambridge."

"Yes, sir. He's the ranch manager. Right up this way. I'll tell him you're here."

The hand ran to the side door and hurried inside. By the time Spur rode to the tie rail near the door, a man came out and offered his hand. He was shorter than average and too fat, and he wore town clothes rather than range attire.

"Loren Cambridge, at your service," he said.

Spur took the hand and shook it. "Spur McCoy,

U.S. Secret Service. Understand you had some trouble here."

"I'm afraid we did. Let's go inside to my office, and I'll tell you everything we know and what we've done."

Inside, Spur saw that the ranch house had been built and furnished with an artistic eye. It would have fit into any Washington or New York expensive neighborhood. The office had been a den with one large window looking out at the far stretch of the prairie to the west.

They sat in upholstered leather armchairs, and when Cambridge offered Spur a cigar from a box, Spur declined. Cambridge took one, bit off the end, lit it and made sure it was burning well. Then he pointed to a map on the wall. It covered the part of western Texas where the Bar-W ranch lay.

Cambridge stood and went to the map. "The home place is here." He touched a spot on the map. "The Sweet Spring River runs through the ranch and northwest. We own all of the water rights on it." He traced a line from the ranch to the northwest.

"We know that the raiders moved up this direction. Our tracking party ran into tracks of a herd that they figured must be well over two hundred being driven northwest.

"We lost the trail in a marshy area and by then figured we were too close to the main summer camp of the band to be prudent, so we returned home. Even if we had found the camp, what could the six of us have done against maybe a hundred Comanche braves?"

Spur lifted his brows. "A hundred is a lot of warriors to be in one band. Hard to find enough grass for their horses when the bands get too large. The average group is from twenty to forty tepees and about that many warrior families."

Cambridge frowned for a moment as if he didn't like to be corrected. "In any event, we returned here and talked to the sheriff. The old man in town hasn't done a damn thing. I wrote the senator about it the night it happened and got it off as a telegram the next day. Of course the senator has little sway over local elected officials."

"It must have worked. The senator called President Grant, who called my boss, who sent me here. Now what else have you done to get the girl back?"

"Nothing. What could we do?"

"You didn't make an offer to ransom her? You could have offered say fifty horses for her. The Comanches value good horses over anything else, even white women."

"Oh, well, I haven't been in this area long enough to know all of the local customs. Cattle are my specialty."

"You didn't check in town to see if there were any half-breeds there who could take an offer to the band or at least find them and see if they would ransom her?"

"No breeds in town I know of. After a raid on an outlying ranch two years ago by the Comanches, the local rednecks ran three breeds out of town and shot a fourth one dead. Don't think you'll find any half-breeds in Sweet Springs."

"Vigilantes?"

"Not really, just a sudden flurry by some rednecks who got scared and went on a tear."

"Where's the closest army post? This should be an army matter, dealing with renegade Indians."

"Hell, the Comanches ain't been sent to a reservation yet. Not a chance to catch these varmints by the army. But guess there is an army post, Fort Griffin, down on the Brazos River, but that's a hundred and fifty miles from here."

"Word should be sent to them about this latest raid. They might come up with some manpower or a company or two to go after the band. That's their job."

"I'll get a letter off tomorrow to the commander of Fort Griffin, but don't think it'll do a diddley damn bit of good."

"So that's about it? That's all I have to work with on this kidnapping?"

"Afraid so. You've been on this kind of a problem before, I'd suspect. I don't see how we can do much more to help you. I'll give you a description of the girl and a picture. Outside of that . . ."

"You had any big rains since the raid?"

"Nothing to talk about. Nothing that would wash out the tracks of the horses. In case you're heading up that way, I'll be glad to send along with you one of the men who went on our ride. He can show you where we lost them and the lay of the land."

"Good. Are any of those six an ex-army man?"

"Yes, Malachi Sully fought in the war. Good man."

"Good. I'll pick him up in the morning here. I need to go back to town and get some basic camp supplies and some food. Have your man bring along enough food for four days on his saddle."

"Can do. Oh, I received a wire from the senator this morning. Came over from Austin by stage. The senator will be arriving in the next two or three days. He wants to help in the search for his daughter."

"Is he an outdoors man?"

"He is. He's been a rancher all his life until he was elected to the senate five years ago. He's tough as barbed wire and twice as reliable. You'll like the senator."

They went outside, and Spur was about to step into his saddle. The sun had dropped to within two fingers of the far horizon, and Spur looked at it. These wide-open vistas always amazed him. He was sure he could see 100 miles due west if the earth's surface didn't curve the way it did. It was an endless horizon.

The sun edged lower.

Four shots almost on top of one another blasted into the silence of the late afternoon. Spur heard a window in the house behind him shatter from a bullet, and he dove to the ground.

"Shots came from the west," Spur shouted.

Cambridge had gone to ground as well. "They're riding right out of the sun," Cambridge said. "Can't see them worth a damn. That's the same way the Indians came a week ago. Wonder if it's the same bastards."

Another window broke behind them. Spur reached up for the Spencer rifle in his scabbard and pumped out seven shots into the sun, where the riders had to be. He heard one scream of protest. A third window in the big ranch house smashed inward from the impact of a bullet; then the distant firing stopped.

Several shots came from the door of the bunkhouse and two shots sounded from one of the barns. Then the afternoon quiet settled down again.

"What'n hell was that?" Spur asked.

Cambridge shrugged.

Spur jumped onto his horse and rode into the sun to see what he could find. Two other horsemen waved at him as he came next to the corral, and they all rode forward.

Ten minutes later they came back. The foreman of the Bar-W, Spur and the third man rode over to where Cambridge waited.

Ed Hunt, the foreman, swung down, his face a mask of controlled fury.

"Cambridge, there's no doubt about it now. We

got them with blood on their damn hands. Those gunshots came from Circle J riders. Some of our shots hit home. There's a dead horse out there with a Circle J brand on him. We've got proof now to take to the sheriff."

"Or to handle ourselves," Cambridge said, his eyes angry, lips pursed. "I'll work out something."

Spur pushed his black hat back on his head. "You're having some trouble with your rancher neighbor?"

Cambridge looked up, his eyes still angry. "Trouble? At least that. Now it's shooting trouble, and I'd say we're just about half a step away from launching a full-scale range war out here. None of your affair. Your job is to find Penny Wallington before those damn Comanches defile her beyond all salvation."

Chapter Three

Spur McCoy stared hard at the ranch manager. "Mr. Cambridge, I don't quite understand what you said about a range war out here not being any of my business. I'm an officer of the court, and that applies to local, state, territorial and unorganized lands. Anything and everything illegal is my business."

Cambridge waved a hand in front of him. "Hey, forget I said that. I'm upset, damned upset. Furious might be a better word. To think that those bastards from the Circle J had the gall to ride in here and shoot some windows out of the house. I've got a short fuse. Everyone knows it. Right now I'd like nothing better than to ride over to the Circle J and burn down a couple of their barns."

"That's the way it starts," Spur said. "I find out you do that or order that done, I'll throw both you and your foreman into the county jail so fast your teeth won't catch up with you for a week. I want your word right now that you won't retaliate. Work up a statement showing the cost of the damage, and I'll take it over to the Circle J with that dead horse when I get back."

He looked hard at the ranch manager. "Agreed, Cambridge?"

"Yeah, agreed."

"Don't do anything until the senator gets here. Then he and I will have a little talk, and we'll head off this range war before it gets started. Just back off."

Spur talked to the man for another 20 minutes, laying out all of the things that had to be done to prevent a shooting war that neither outfit could possibly win. He capped it with a clincher.

"Remember, Cambridge, this isn't your ranch, and it isn't your money that you'd be putting on the line in a range war. It probably wouldn't even be your life that would be in the shooting front lines. I'll see you in the morning."

It took Spur a little over an hour to ride back to Sweet Springs. He put the mount in the livery, told them he'd want it again the next morning at 6:30 and headed for the first cafe that he found. It was across from the bank and had six tables and stools along a counter.

Spur had roast beef with a creamy horseradish sauce that took the top of his head right through the ceiling. A woman sitting at the table next to his grinned when he yelped and grabbed for a glass of water. He hit the edge of the glass, which jolted off the table, broke on the wooden floor and splashed water on the woman's shoes and skirt.

Spur left his chair and picked up the broken glass at the woman's feet.

"Sorry about the clumsiness," he said. "Did the broken glass cut you?"

She looked down smiling. It was a great smile.

She had brown hair and a round face, and she was laughing.

"Not hurt, just a little wet, but I dry off real good. Was it the horseradish?"

"It was."

Spur picked up the rest of the broken glass and put it on his table. She sipped her coffee, her meal finished.

"You're new in town," she said.

"True. Does everyone here know everyone else?"

"Just about. Mind if I join you to finish my coffee?"

"I'd be pleased. I hate to eat alone."

"You probably don't have to unless you want to."

When she stood up he checked her slender form— tight little bottom, small waist, dress pressed tight over her big breasts. About 30 years old, he figured. She sat down across from him, and for a moment her knee touched his under the table.

"Oh, sorry," she said. "The roast beef is good."

"It is." Spur hesitated, then held out his hand. "I'm Spur McCoy, stranger in town."

She grinned, showing even white teeth, and shook his hand. "I'm Tory, really Victoria, but I like Tory better."

"Good, I like that name, Tory. Lived here a long time?"

"Forever. I want to get away and go to Austin, but Daddy doesn't want me to go. I feel hemmed in here, restricted."

"I don't see any wedding ring."

"Nope, I'm an old maid." She paused. "Well, in a manner of speaking. You're not wearing a ring either."

"True." He didn't elaborate and went on eating. When he finished he knew that she worked at her father's bank, that her last name was Roth, and that

29

she had a small house of her own not far from her father's place.

"Would you mind if I walked you home?"

She shook her head. "Wouldn't work. Too many people would see us and start talking."

One of her hands under the table found his knee, and she rubbed it and moved up his inner thigh.

"You staying at the hotel?"

"The Palace."

"What room?"

He barely heard her words. Her hand edged higher up his thigh.

"Room two-twelve. Are you sure?"

"If I'm not sure, I won't be there. You go right back. Might take me a few minutes."

Spur stood up and paid his bill. The man behind the counter said nothing about the broken glass or Spur's talk with Tory Roth.

It took him five minutes to get back to the hotel. There were no messages in box 212, so he took his key and went up to his room. He went inside the way he always did. Spur stood at the doorknob side against the wall, reached out and unlocked the door. Nothing happened. He pushed the panel hard so it swung and hit the wall inside. No one hiding behind the door.

It wasn't dark yet. He peered around the door frame and saw that no one lurked inside the room. Inside he pulled the blind down behind the thin white curtains, lit the lamp and moved his gear off the bed.

He would go to the general store in the morning for a few pots and dishes and some trail food. Then he'd be on his way to track down the senator's daughter. If he made any Indian contact, he'd offer 50 horses and go up to 100 if he had to. Horses were far more important to the Comanches than captive white women.

He had just pushed his carpetbag under the bed, lifted off his gunbelt and hung it over the bedstead headboard post, when a faint knock sounded on the door.

He opened it, and Tory slipped in. She wore a floppy straw hat that nearly covered her face. He closed the door and locked it, then put the straight chair under the doorknob. Anyone trying to break in would have to break the chair first.

Spur nodded. "Looks like you're sure."

Tory lifted off the hat and sailed it onto the bed.

"Look, I don't know what you're thinking. I don't go around going to hotel rooms with every stranger who comes to town. With you it's different. I like your looks, your style, the way you walk, the way you talk. You treat me like a lady even though you don't know me from President Grant's wife, Julia." She watched him and sighed.

"Maybe this was a mistake. You want me to walk out?"

He tipped her chin up and kissed her lips gently. Her eyes closed, and a long sigh escaped from her when the kiss ended.

"Oh, my, I think I'll stay. But you'll have to kiss me that way again."

Spur kissed her again, pulling her tightly against his chest so her breasts pressed against him. Her hand went to his crotch and felt around until she found the hardness growing. When the kiss ended he kept holding her and walked her to the bed. Spur looked at her, and she nodded.

"Oh, God, yes! It's been so long. I used to be married, and I loved making love with my husband. I know some women who hate to spread their legs, but I couldn't get enough of it. I guess that's how

I found out I was unable to conceive, so my man left me."

When Spur let go of her, they sat on the bed, their legs and their sides touching. He kissed her again, then trailed small kisses down her neck to the open throat of her dress. She undid the buttons, and he nosed lower until he found the rise of a breast.

"Oh, God, please, Spur McCoy. Please kiss me there."

He undid the rest of the top of her dress, pulled up the chemise and found her throbbing breasts. They had narrow areolas and nipples bright red with new blood, surging with each heartbeat.

He kissed one breast, and she jumped, then smiled as her hands played with his longish dark hair.

"Sweet little darling, just do that forever. It makes me feel like I'm a real woman again, not just some teller in a small bank in some damn village in Texas. Makes me feel like a real woman."

He kissed her nipple and she gasped; then he licked it until she moaned softly. When he nibbled at her nipple she shivered, threw her arms around him and pulled him backward onto the bed as her body jolted into a series of spasms that pounded her hips against him and rattled her whole body. She gasped for breath, but at once another series of shocks hit her body as she wailed and moaned and reached for his lips, kissing him so hard his lips hurt.

The climax scorched her once more, then left her panting and exhausted. She rolled away from him, curling into a fetal ball.

"No," she said softly, "I can't let you. I'm halfway respectable, even if I am divorced. Half the women in town still talk to me. If this ever gets around . . ." She stopped. Slowly she straightened out and turned back to him.

"Oh, damn, but that was so fine. Forget what I said. I want you deep inside me so bad I can even say fuck." Her eyes went wide a moment, and she smiled. "Yes, Spur McCoy, I can tell you I want you to fuck me long and hard and all night. Maybe my ex-husband was the sterile one, not me at all. If I got pregnant I'd prove it to him, wouldn't I?"

She sat up, freed the dress from under her and pulled it over her head. Then she took off the chemise and sat there only in her short bloomers, which came halfway to her knees.

She reached over and felt the long bulge under his pants. "Oh, good, you still want me, Spur McCoy." She worked on his belt, loosening it, then undid the buttons down his fly. He helped her, pulling off his boots, then sliding down his pants and kicking them away.

Tory stared at the bulge in his short underwear. Her hands touched it, then pulled away. In a swift move she caught his underwear and pulled it down, taking care to lift it over his erection. When his prick leaped out of the cloth she shrieked, and her eyes went wide.

"Oh, my! He's twice the size of my ex-husband's. I'm thinking more and more he was the reason I couldn't get pregnant."

She looked up at him. "I'm not a good judge—what I mean is I've only been with two men in my whole life, him and you—so I don't know how big . . ." She blushed. "You know what I mean."

Spur chuckled and caressed her breasts. "Yes, I know what you mean. There's no standard size. Kind of like a woman's breasts, whatever is big enough to do the job."

"Oh, glory, I bet he can do the job." She pulled his underwear off his feet, then took off his jacket and shirt until he was naked.

Spur reached for her bloomers, but she caught his hand. "Not quite yet. It's been a long time. I need a little more encouragement."

He kissed her, then pulled her body on top of his.

"Oh, I like it up here. He'd never let me do this."

Spur edged her higher until she could drop a breast into his mouth. He kissed it, then gulped in as much of the big orb as he could and tenderly chewed on it.

"Glory, nobody's ever done that before. Makes me feel all sexy and hot and wet down below. Damn but that feels great!"

He worked over her other breast the same way, then took her hand and placed it around his stiff shaft.

"Spur McCoy, I'm so glad I decided to eat out tonight instead of cooking my supper at home. I'm also delighted that you knocked over your glass of water."

Spur moved his mouth from her breast and smiled. "I'm glad, too."

He rolled her off and worked one hand slowly up her inner thigh. It was like listening to a steam engine getting up power. Her breathing came faster and faster, her breath like a blast of hot steam on his neck.

His fingers worked almost to her crotch, then jumped to the other side and massaged downward.

"Come back," she said softly, her voice a throaty growl. "Touch me there, please, Spur. Please touch my tender little cuntie."

He pressed the damp spot at her crotch, and she moaned in delight. Her hand caught his and took it to the waist of her bloomers. Together they pulled them down and off her feet.

"Touch me again, Spur."

He did and found her wet and ready, her juices trailing down her legs in anticipation. He petted her outer lips, and when he brushed across her clit, she jolted.

"No, I want you inside me, right now," she said. Her voice came soft and low, so charged with desire and emotion that it didn't sound like her at all.

She lifted her knees and spread them, then opened her arms for him and nodded.

Spur slid between her thighs and watched her.

"Oh, yes, please, right now before I explode."

He knelt and moved forward. Her eager hands directed him, and he edged into her juicy slot.

"Oh, yes!" she keened, high and soft. "Yes, yes, all the way in," she whispered.

Spur felt her juices lubricating him, and he drove forward until their pelvic bones ground together.

Tory let out one cry of pain and delight, then threw her arms around him, her hips dancing against his. Tears glistened in her eyes as she gasped for air.

Spur balanced his weight on his elbows and stroked into her gently at first. Then her hips rose to meet his with such force that he worked harder and faster until he realized that he was beyond control.

Tory shrieked in delight as she realized that he was about to climax. She pounded harder and he worked faster until the whole world exploded in his head. His hips jolted a dozen times, and then he collapsed on top of her, driving her into the mattress with his weight.

They lay there for five minutes as he recuperated. Her eyes were wide, staring at him.

"So that's what it's supposed to be like. He never could go all the way. He said it hurt or something. He never shot inside me the way you did. Amazing!"

Spur laughed softly, getting his wind back. "Sweet Tory, I don't think you'll have any trouble at all getting pregnant when you get together with a real man. Your husband must have had the problem, not you."

She hugged him so tight he thought she would cut off his breath. She squirmed under him, and he rolled away and lay beside her.

"You really think it was his problem?"

"Sounds like it."

Her smile was so beautiful he wanted to preserve it for all time. A light came on in her eyes that he was sure wouldn't go out for the rest of her life.

"Oh, glory! Now that I know what the matter was, I can hold my head up again. I can find a man who loves me and raise a family. Oh, Spur McCoy, I hope you realize just how important that is to me right now."

He told her he did.

"Again, wonderful Spur McCoy."

He chuckled. "Hey, you have to give me at least fifteen minutes to get my strength back."

"I'll give you ten minutes, no more. There are just ever so many sexy and wonderful things I want to try before the night is over."

They tried them all.

It was slightly after six A.M. when someone banged on his door.

"McCoy? You in there?"

Spur awoke slowly, got out of bed and saw that Tory still slept. He went to the door and opened it a crack.

"Spur McCoy?"

"Yeah."

"You better come right out to the Bar-W ranch. We've got trouble. Last night three Circle J riders came in and burned down the second barn. Our man on guard shot one of the attackers and killed him. He's Jed Matthews. He worked at the Circle J spread. Mr. Cambridge wants you to come out to the ranch just as soon as you can."

"Damn," Spur said. "Sounds like the range war has started."

Chapter Four

Spur dressed quickly, took his six-gun, a change of clothes and rode with the cowhand toward the Bar-W ranch without stopping at the general store for any gear or provisions. They pushed the horses and got to the ranch house slightly after seven. The place was an armed camp.

Two cowhands with rifles met them at the head of the lane and made sure who they were before letting them in.

Cambridge was unshaven, looked as if he'd been up all night and carried a six-gun in new-looking leather.

"I've got guards out on all four sides of the ranch buildings," Cambridge said. "We've dusted off every weapon on the place including six shotguns. Every man has a rifle and a hundred rounds. Hell, it looks like a war is on already, and the shooting isn't more than six hours old."

"How far to the Circle J?" Spur asked.

"About fifteen miles."

"Get your horse. We're going for a ride. Oh, was there any identification on the dead man?"

"Hell, yes. His change purse had two letters addressed to him from Michigan."

"Bring that along, and let's get moving."

Cambridge stared at him. "Can I bring my six-gun and a rifle?"

"No, not knowing your state of mind. I'll be armed, and I'll be doing the talking. Now let's ride."

They put the horses into a lope and averaged six miles an hour. The ride to the Circle J took a little over two and a half hours, and they arrived just after ten A.M. There was no rifle-toting guard at the lane that led back to the Circle J spread.

Spur had cautioned Cambridge during half the ride.

"Just sit there and be quiet. I've been in these situations before, and I'm an impartial party. I'm also the law, and that's going to carry a lot of weight. Whatever you do don't blow up, don't get angry, and don't start yelling and threatening anyone."

As they approached the ranch house, a large man wearing a gun and carrying a shotgun came out the back door and stood on the step. He was over six feet tall, and Spur figured he weighed nearly 300 pounds. He wore a battered brown Stetson and a full red beard.

"That's Ray Jordan who owns this spread," Cambridge said softly so the big man on the steps couldn't hear.

The two riders came to a halt ten yards from the back steps where Jordan stood.

"Cambridge, nobody said you could set foot on my spread. What are you doing here?"

"Mr. Jordan, my name is Spur McCoy. I'm a United States Secret Service Agent. You've probably heard of U.S. Marshals. I pack about ten times the lawman power that a U.S. Marshal does. Before you do or say anything incriminating, I think we should sit down and have a talk."

"You bringing the law into this, Cambridge?"

"He didn't bring me, Mr. Jordan. I brought him. I'm in the area to help find the senator's kidnapped daughter. This is just extra work for me, so don't go out of your way to get me riled. Do you want to talk here or from the other side of the bars down at the county jail?"

"Huh? All right, I can talk good as the next man."

They went to the porch and sat around an outdoor table that had been painted a half-dozen times, showing splotches of various colors.

When they had settled down, Spur held up his hand. "Now, I know there's some problems between your two spreads. I don't have time to work that out right now. All I can do now is make sure nothing more happens like did yesterday over at the Bar-W."

"What the hell was that?" Jordan asked.

"You know what it was, Mr. Jordan. I won't put up with any smart talk from either one of you, so just simmer down. I was on the site when a number of your men rode out of the setting sun and shot out half a dozen windows from the ranch house there. We returned fire and killed one of your horses. It carries your brand, and don't give me any shit about it being a stray somebody found. What do you have to say about this act of attempted murder?"

"Murder? Just some of my boys having some fun."

"Fine, they can stand charges and have fun with three to five years in Texas State Prison. We have a statement of charges for damage to the ranch house and ammunition expended. The total comes to thirty-seven dollars and forty-five cents."

Jordan nodded, a grin slipping onto his full face. "Reckon I can stand them charges. I don't admit it was my men who did it. Just settle it to be neighborly."

"Fine. Now later that same night or early this morning, the large barn at the Bar-W ranch caught fire and burned to the ground. A guard saw five men light the fire in the barn, rush out, mount and ride away. The guard fired seven shots and hit one of the arsonists.

"That man is Jed Matthews, who rides for you. He's currently still at the Bar-W."

"You shot Jed? Hell, he was just funnin'."

"Burning down a barn is arson, Mr. Jordan, and draws a sentence of from five to ten years in prison. I want the names of the other four men so they can be put on trial as soon as possible in Sweet Springs."

"How would I know who they are?"

"They work for you, and they rode at your direction. I'm sure you know who they are."

"I guess I could find out," Jordan said, the grin gone now, a pained expression replacing it.

"There also is a statement of charges for the burned-down barn, the death of two milk cows, the loss of ten tons of cut hay, replacement of a buggy and the cost of rebuilding the barn. It comes to $2,486."

Jordan scooted his chair back and quickly stood up. "What the hell? No barn is worth that much. I built one last year for two hundred dollars."

"This is the cost of rebuilding this barn, Mr. Jordan, replacing the buggy and the two cows. Are you prepared to repay the Bar-W now, or will that have to go to civil court?"

"Robbery, but I can pay."

"Now, how about the names of those other four men who burned down the barn."

Jordan gave the names of the men.

Spur stood. "I'd say this meeting is nearly over. Oh, you haven't inquired into the condition of your rider, Matthews."

Jordan had remained standing. His fists came on his hips, and he glared at Spur. "Figured you'd tell me in your own time."

"I will. Matthews was shot dead last night. You may not know it, Jordan, but when a death occurs during the commission of a felony, all participants can be charged with murder. Those four riders of yours will be charged with murder just as soon as I can get back to town and talk with the district attorney in this county. I'd suggest you advise none of them to take any long trips."

"You . . . you can't do that. It ain't right."

"Neither is burning down your neighbor's barn, Mr. Jordan, or getting your rider shot to death. I'd advise that you undertake no further acts of violence against the Bar-W. If you have anything further to say, you should talk to the county district attorney."

Spur turned his back on the rancher, and he and Cambridge walked to their horses. For a moment Spur felt a tickle at the back of his neck, but it passed. He figured that Jordan had almost drawn his six-gun but didn't.

The two men leisurely rode away from the Circle J. Once out of easy rifle range, they picked the pace up to a lope and headed for the Bar-W.

Cambridge was grinning so wide it nearly split his face open.

"Damn! Never saw old Jordan so caught in his own trap. He was steamed and fixing to explode there when you hit him with them four murder charges. Can you really do that?"

"Most certainly, Mr. Cambridge. It's basic common law. Not done too often, but it works as a great threat. I don't think you'll have any more problems with the Circle J, at least until I get back from the hunt for Penny Wallington. That man of yours ready to go?"

"Yes, I told him last night."

"I didn't have time to get any camp gear. We'll need a pot or two off your chuck wagon and enough trail food for the two of us for four or five days. Hard telling how long we'll be gone."

Back at the Bar-W three hours later, Spur put his saddle on a new mount from the ranch and loaded the gear and food on the two nags.

The man who would be going with him was Malachi Sully—a short man, no more than five-five. He was Texas-thin, wore a high-crowned brown Stetson and carried a six-gun on each hip.

They rode at a steady walk. Sully figured they had 70 miles to travel to the swampy area.

"Long damn ways, Spur," Sully said. "We spent two hard days going each way before."

"We should figure on getting as far as we can tonight," Spur said. "Maybe ride until ten o'clock before we stop. You have any trouble following the trail?"

"Hard to miss, even in the dark," Sully said.

They rode until eleven that night, then rolled out their blankets and made a cold camp. Any smoke this far north could be seen or smelled by some roving hunter from the Comanche camp. Spur figured they had gone about 25 miles and still had a lot of ground to cover.

The second day the tracks were harder to follow. Evidently a local thunderstorm had swept through the area, and in places the tracks of the large number of horses were completely wiped out. They followed the general direction of the march and soon found the tracks again, but they had wasted two hours.

Late that second night, they came to the spot where the first tracking party had turned around.

"This is the place," Sully said. "They drove the horses through the marshy place. That's the only way up through here, so I don't think they were trying to foil any trackers."

They camped there that night, made a small cooking fire and had bacon and sausages sandwiches and a can each of sliced peaches. Sliced peaches had quickly become a favorite dessert on the range, especially on short trips where weight was not a big problem.

With first light, they were up and moving. Spur worked through the marsh and found the horse tracks plainly on the far side, moving on up the valley that seemed to lead to some kind of a small pass ahead.

Now they had come close enough to see in the distance the abrupt bluff that soared hundreds of feet into the air. Spur had heard the great barrier cliff went along for 200 miles.

"The Staked Plains is right up there the other side of that bluff," Sully said. "I've never been this close to them before."

"You don't suppose the band lives up there?"

Sully shook his head. "Not in the summer. They come over here from somewhere to hunt and gather nuts and berries. Nothing grows up there."

They walked their mounts now, watching ahead. Three miles farther up the wide valley Spur sniffed. "Wood smoke," he said. "We must be downwind from the big camp. We'll find a place to hide out during the rest of the day and move up in the dark and see what kind of a camp they have."

"We going to try to get Penny out of there?" Sully asked.

"Two of us against a hundred warriors or even fifty? Not good odds if you want to live to a ripe old age. First we'll scout out the place."

As soon as it was dark, they left their thick brushy hideaway and walked their horses upstream. The night showed half a moon and made their movements easier.

The smell of wood smoke became stronger, and when they rounded a bend in the stream, they could see dozens of fires burning ahead.

They tied off their horses and slipped up closer. When they were still half a mile away, Spur began counting the tepees. He came up with 44 or 45; he wasn't sure which.

Sully shook his head. "I ain't going no closer. I don't want to get buried up to my neck in an anthill. I heard about them."

Spur prodded him. "We won't get caught. They don't expect anyone. They don't even have lookouts on duty. You're as safe as you would be in your grandmother's living room."

They had moved closer to the cliff of the Staked Plains. Spur worked up the side of a rock fall so they could see the camp better. Yes, 45 tepees, which should mean about 45 warriors. One of the tepees seemed larger than the rest. It had a huge fire dancing in front of it, and what appeared to be some kind of a council was in session.

The flames revealed a large flying eagle painted on one side of the big tepee. It had to be the tribe's leader. The only Comanche chief Spur could remember was Flying Eagle, a man of about 40 who had won all sorts of honors as a warrior leader.

Flying Eagle's band was the biggest horse trading

group among the Comanches. He'd trade horse for anything, anywhere. He'd trade for them if he couldn't steal them.

Yes, the trade had to be horses for Penny.

They stayed for three hours watching the camp. Finally the council broke up, most of the fires died out, and the Comanche camp lay quiet with most of the Indians sleeping. Spur watched carefully, but the only thing he saw moving around the camp were the dogs.

That was when Spur was glad they were downwind from the camp. He hadn't seen any sign of a white woman. She was probably in a tepee somewhere. Whether she was going to be a wife or a slave to the warrior who captured her, the first few sexual encounters would be about the same—rough, demanding, perhaps brutal.

Spur sighed. There was nothing he could do about Penny Wallington right now, U.S. senator's daughter or no. He could stay where he was, create a better screen for himself and watch the camp during daylight. Maybe then he could spot the girl.

He rejected that idea quickly. Too risky. He had nothing to bargain with for the captive. He'd much rather have a company of horse soldiers behind him on that kind of mission. Spur decided he'd done all he could for now. He'd get back to the ranch, and by then the senator might have arrived and they could make some plans. Maybe the senator could get some army troops from Fort Griffin. Maybe he had already had a troop on the march to meet him at the ranch. Spur could only hope.

Spur woke up Sully, and they withdrew to their horses, then started the long ride back to the Bar-W ranch. The senator wasn't going to be happy with what Spur had to tell him.

He was sure that Penny wasn't happy. She'd been

in the savages' hands now for two weeks. It would be some time before they could even try to rescue her. He wished her well, all 18 years of her. Spur felt he was involved in a tragedy, and he felt helpless because he didn't know what to do about it.

Chapter Five

Penny Wallington could never remember being so absolutely filthy. She had not been allowed to take a bath or even wash in the small stream since she had arrived ten days before. Her hair was terrible, matted and filthy. She had to sleep on the ground on nothing more than an old buffalo robe.

She sat outside the tepee, grateful at least that she could be in the clean mountain air. It was hot, but at least she was outside. For the first three days they had kept her inside the shelter all the time except for occasional trips to relieve herself.

Wantabe's second wife, the younger pregnant one, had been the least angry and savage toward her. She went with Penny to relieve herself and made sure she didn't get away. Penny figured she could easily outrun the girl who must be seven months pregnant, but the warriors would soon come and find her.

She sat slightly behind and to the left of Wantabe, the warrior who had captured her. Penny wasn't sure what he was doing, but she had the idea that he was showing her off, offering her for sale. Two other warriors had stopped by, stared at her, commented to Wantabe and moved on. Soon an older man came. He, like the other warriors, wore only a breechclout, no shirt or pants.

She was getting used to it by now, but at first all of that male bare flesh embarrassed her.

The older man chattered with Wantabe a moment, then knelt down beside her and lifted her dress to look at her legs, then caught her breasts as if measuring them. She almost slapped the old man, but Wantabe growled at her. At last the older Indian warrior had shaken his head and left.

Penny thought back to that first night in the tepee when Wantabe had forced himself on her. He was larger than she was and so strong it amazed her. He had spread her legs and jammed into her searing dry flesh, leaving a hurt that hadn't healed yet.

For years she had dreamed of making love for the first time. One of the girls in Washington, D.C., had done it several times and told Penny in intimate detail what happened and how it felt. Penny figured that the girl was pregnant by now and hunting for a husband.

Penny had stopped struggling when Wantabe was inside her. She could do nothing then. Gradually her juices flowed, and his thrusting became easier. For a few moments it seemed right and natural, and then he grunted and bellowed and thrust hard six times into her.

Then he pulled away, left her and went to eat. Penny lay where he had left her. Was that all there was to it? She had felt nothing but pain and then the start of a soft warm glow when he finished and left. She put her dress back on and went toward the cooking fire at the center of the tepee.

The older woman, Wantabe's number one wife, shouted at her and motioned her to go back. Wantabe was eating. She had the idea that he ate first, and if there was anything left, the wives would share it. Or perhaps she would be last to eat and there would be none left at all.

The second day there she caught the names of the two wives. The older one was Heypau. Penny had no idea what the name meant. She thought Indians had romantic names such as Little Deer and Running Fawn. The pregnant girl, who Penny figured was no more than 16 or 17 years old, was called Flanroo. The words were Comanche and again meant nothing to her. She said them over and over so she could use them when she had to. Wantabe was the other name she would never forget.

Twice more Wantabe had come to her blankets and taken her. She found it far easier not to fight him. The second time he had hit her in the face, slapping her to the side when she was slow pulling off her dress.

That time it was light enough to see his erection. It was shorter than she thought it must be from the way it entered her and reddish and purple with the nearly hairless sack below where his balls were. The girl in Washington had told her all about a man's privates and even drew pictures for her. Still it was a shock and a surprise.

Would she ever be clean again? Wantabe rose from where he sat outside his tepee. To his left his lance rested against a small tree, and beside it stood his shield made of tough buffalo hide. It had some strange drawings and colored splotches on it. Both stood there ready for instant use in case of attack.

Penny was surprised how hard the women worked. They had the jobs of cooking the food or bringing in firewood, doing all of the tasks around the camp. She had heard that when the tepees were taken down for a move, the women did all that work, too, packing everything and loading it.

The warriors and older boys did nothing during the day. The men vanished now and then and sometimes came back with deer or antelope. Then the happy warrior's family butchered the animal, cut up the meat, parceled out some to friends and cooked a lot of it. The rest they cut in thin strips and hung on racks made of sharp-pointed pegs. The meat would take three days of warm sun to dry enough so it would not spoil. It became venison jerky. When it was dry it was stored carefully in parfleches.

These were rectangular boxes made of rawhide and used to store food and pemmican and jerky. She had found the one holding the family's jerky and stole a small piece and chewed on it. The dried meat was quite delicious.

Now she watched as Wantabe finished eating and left. She had figured he was in his middle twenties. His first wife looked to be about the same age. There were no children. Evidently Heypau was unable to bring forth.

So now Wantabe had a second brood mare to provide him with many children. No, she wouldn't bear him a child. She was too young to be pregnant. She wanted to go home and then back to Washington and to her school!

Flanroo motioned to her and scooped stew from a boiling bag over the low fire. She used a horn spoon and put the food in a bowl made from a gourd that had been hardened in a fire.

Penny had gone from revulsion at the very sight and taste of the Indian food to getting so hungry that she ate anything she could find or that they gave her. Tonight's meal was almost meatless. What little meat was in the soup could have been squirrel. That wasn't so bad. Being a Texan she'd eaten squirrel before as well as rattlesnake and once some antelope.

After she ate, they gave her the gourds and the boiling sack to wash in the small stream. Flanroo went with her and watched. When it all was clean, Penny sat beside the stream, tossing rocks into the water.

Flanroo came and sat beside her. She smiled for the first time Penny could remember. She motioned with her hands, but Penny didn't understand.

Flanroo frowned a moment. "Wantabe," she said. Penny watched her. "Wantabe," she said again, then hit her palms together; one stayed close but the other one moved outward.

Flanroo did it twice.

Penny frowned, trying to understand. "Wantabe," Penny said, then did the same motion with her hands.

Flanroo nodded and smiled. Penny did it again and this time said, "Wantabe go."

Flanroo looked up at the new word. Penny repeated it. At last Flanroo tried it and after three tries got it right. It was the first word of English that Penny taught the pregnant Indian girl.

Penny shivered that night as Wantabe came into the tepee. He stared at her in the soft light of the fire, then sat down on the low pallet and stroked her breasts through the dress. When a call came from outside he growled, rose and went out. He didn't come back all night.

The next morning Wantabe was gone. Flanroo motioned with her hands and tried to explain where the warrior was. At last Penny understood. He was with six other warriors on a long hunt. They went with their horses and would be gone two to three days.

Life around the tepee was easier that day. When evening came they ate cooked jerky and berries they had picked. Night settled in, and the three women went to their buffalo robes. Penny was farthest back in the tepee, against the outer skin of the shelter that had been rolled up a foot to allow the soft cooling breezes to blow through.

She settled down in her robes and tried to go to sleep. A moment later she heard Heypau snoring softly on the other side of the brightly burning fire.

Penny looked up with a start as Flanroo eased down beside her. Flanroo talked softly to Penny, who hadn't the slightest idea what she said. Penny slept in her one dress, realizing that it was now grimy and torn, but she had nothing else.

Flanroo urged Penny to sit up, and she lifted up a soft doeskin dress from the ground. Penny smiled and nodded in the low light from the fire.

Flanroo touched her chest and then pointed to Penny and handed her the dress. It must be a present from Flanroo—a real dress made of tough doeskin. It would be much more practical than what she was wearing.

Penny nodded and in a rush of emotion reached out and hugged the Indian girl. Flanroo hugged her back. When they parted, Flanroo held up her hand. She took back the dress and touched her chest again, then touched Penny.

"What?" Penny asked, not understanding.

Then Flanroo's hand cupped Penny's breast and fondled it. The touch was so gentle that Penny didn't know what to do. Slowly the realization broke through to her. She had heard from her friend in Washington that some women made love with other women. They had joked about it, wondering just who did what. Now it was no joke.

Penny stiffened, but Flanroo paid no attention. She caressed Penny's breasts, and at once Penny realized that they were becoming warmer, that her nipples were hardening and rising. She had never felt this way before in her life.

Penny sat there, frozen now, unable to move. Flanroo seemed to know what to do. She lifted the white woman's dress over her head and laid it aside; then she caught Penny's bare breasts in each hand and fondled them and caressed them until Penny sensed that her body was responding, that she was breathing faster.

Flanroo caught one of Penny's hands and slipped it under her doeskin dress and up to her swelling breasts. The Indian woman muttered a few words, and Penny rubbed the breast gently. Slowly, Flanroo eased Penny back until she lay on her robes. One of the Indian woman's hands pushed down to Penny's crotch and lay there. Gently Flanroo brushed her hand over Penny's most private place.

Penny whimpered. It was so gentle, so tender. Penny felt the woman's mouth cover one of her breasts and chew tenderly; then her tongue licked Penny's breast.

Penny gasped as the woman's finger pressed into her vagina. It came out a moment later, then sought a place just above and rubbed gently.

The tiny bud of Penny's clit twanged one way and then the other and Penny's eyes went wide, her breath gushing out in a furious panting. Then before she knew what happened, her whole body shook and jolted. It felt like every nerve ending in her body had been charged with electricity, and she responded with a shivering and shaking as spasms ripped through her. It all happened so quickly, and then it was over.

Penny realized that she was sweating, that her body was reacting to the woman's finger.

Then Flanroo caught Penny's hand and drew it to her own crotch around her distended belly. Penny let her hand lay there. Flanroo said something, took Penny's hand and pushed it at her outer labia. Penny gasped.

Flanroo said something else, softly and gently. She took Penny's hand, extended two fingers and pushed them into Flanroo's vagina.

"Oh, my!" Penny said.

Flanroo urged her to thrust them in and out like a penis, and she did so a dozen times. Then the Indian woman moved Penny's finger to her clit and taught Penny how to twang it back and forth.

Penny frowned in the darkness. The Indian had her sitting up then with one hand caressing her breast and the other strumming her clit. It took longer, but soon Flanroo shrilled softly. Her body spasmed the way Penny's had, and she shook and rattled and moaned as the climax tore through her.

When it was over, Flanroo slid into the bed beside Penny, drawing the soft buffalo robes over them. She kissed Penny's breasts, clutched at Penny's crotch with her hand and then whispered something Penny didn't understand. A moment later the Indian woman went to sleep.

Penny had learned a lot in this Indian camp. She'd have a thing or two to tell Belle back in Washington if she ever saw her again.

Penny felt the woman's hand on her breast and smiled. She reached over and caressed the pregnant Indian woman's breast until she stirred; then she put her hand between the woman's legs. Flanroo parted her legs, and Penny rubbed her clit again until Flanroo woke up climaxing. She laughed softly, grinned and then tore into the last part of her climax.

The only thing that didn't seem to be affected by the exchange of caresses was Heypau, who kept up her usual snoring until both the young girls went to sleep.

When Penny awoke in the morning, Flanroo was gone. Penny frowned for a moment wondering if it had been a dream. Then she realized that she was naked under the buffalo robes. Maybe it wasn't a dream.

She looked around in the light of the new day and saw the doeskin dress lying at the foot of her pallet. Penny sat up in a rush. It wasn't a dream. Now she was certain that she had a good friend in the Comanche camp.

Penny thought about it. In the nearly two weeks she had lived here, she had never once seen Wantabe talk to or even touch Flanroo. He ignored her. She decided it must be some part of Indian culture so he wouldn't put a hex on the new child. But Flanroo had wanted some tenderness. Penny nodded. Who had it hurt? She had learned something new about her own body, and she had given the poor girl some tenderness.

That decided, Penny stood, slipped the new dress over her head and smiled. Yes, it would be a fine dress for her as long as she had to stay here. Now, just where was her father and all of those army troops he said he used to command? Maybe she would have to try to get out of here by herself. An idea began to form in the back of her mind. It could work, but she'd need some help. If Flanroo would help her, she just might be able to do it!

Chapter Six

The ride back from the rim of the Staked Plains was uneventful. It took them a full two days, and they arrived at the Bar-W tired and grouchy. United States Senator Wyman B. Wallington stood on the back porch, smoking a cigar and watching them ride in.

Spur dropped off the horse as soon as he saw the imposing figured and walked up to him. The senator was six feet tall and broad shouldered. He wore range clothes and a gunbelt with a well-worn Colt sticking out of leather. His fists were doubled up on his hips as he stared at Spur. As Spur walked up to him he saw that the senator's face was rugged and aging; his blue eyes snapped, and he had a crown of gray and black hair that looked like it didn't like to be combed. He grabbed the cigar out of his mouth and puffed out the smoke.

"Senator Wallington, Spur McCoy. I'm with the

U.S. Secret Service, and General Halleck sent me out here to help find Penny."

"McCoy," the senator said holding out his hand. "I've heard some damn fine things about you. Hope they're true and that you can work some of your magic for Penny's sake."

"I hope so, too, Senator. Let me wash up and get a cup of coffee and I'll tell you everything I know about her situation."

"You had anything to eat?" Spur shook his head. "Fine, we'll talk in the kitchen after you've eaten. I know there's nothing we can do this instant, even though I'd like to."

A half hour later the senator eyed Spur over the big table in the large kitchen where the family and help took their meals. The kitchen had two stoves at one side, a big ice box, standing chopping block, tables and cabinets. A fireplace on the other side was near the table.

"So, McCoy, let's talk. Cambridge, my manager here, filled me in. I'll take over things now. He'll stay in the background, and you might not see him again. He likes his little office. Now, do you think the Comanches will trade?"

"They trade for horses more than any other Comanche band, and the Comanches are the biggest horse stealers and traders in the country. I'd say they will trade for Penny."

"How many?"

"I'd start with thirty-five and go up to a hundred if we have to."

"That's no problem. I'll buy horses if I run out. What's the procedure?"

"Senator, I've dealt with a lot of Indians. Most of them don't hold with palaver. They want action. They believe what they can see and touch, not in promises. I'd say our best bet is to drive fifty horses up that valley with enough men to protect them; then I'll ride into their camp with no weapons and have a talk."

"You could wind up full of arrows or sliced into bits."

"True. But the Comanche warrior respects a man who shows bravery, who is outrageous in showing it, and who can fight."

"You'll have to fight them?"

"At least one of them. If I can prove that I can stand up to their best warrior, we'll have a chance."

"Why not just charge in there with two companies of cavalry from Fort Griffin and take back Penny?"

Spur sighed. This might be harder than he thought it would be. He could have two fights on his hands, one here and one at the Comanche camp. He shook his head and looked hard at the senator.

"Won't work if you want to see your daughter alive. Comanches are strange about that. Ask any army man, and he'll tell you. The first thing the Comanche women do when the army attacks them is to kill any white slave or white wife in her tepee. It's almost automatic. Penny wouldn't last more than two or three minutes if you attack that camp with cavalry."

The senator stood, clasped his hands behind his back and paced back and forth from the table to the stove. He made the circuit five times, then stopped near where Spur sat sipping his third cup of coffee.

"You think you can do what three hundred cavalry troopers can't do? Is that what you're telling me?"

Spur nodded. "Not exactly. I'm saying we have a good chance to get Penny out alive and unharmed if I go in with fifty horses to trade. I'm saying that if you send in the army, I won't go along. I don't like to bury white girls slaughtered in a Comanche camp. I've seen it before, Senator. I have no hankering to look at what those squaws do to a captive white woman they have hated ever since their warrior brought her back from some raid. Most warriors have two or three wives, and they are all excellent at using knives."

Senator Wallington sat down in a chair across the plank table. "All right, McCoy, I understand. I'll have to change my way of thinking. These people are savages, and I have to remember that. They live for the moment and live by their senses, not by their intellect. Yes, I have it.

"I just thank God that the President had them send you. Now, what's our schedule? When can you go back up there? How many men will you need?"

Before Spur could answer a man rushed into the kitchen. He was Ed Hunt, the Bar-W foreman. He looked at Spur and the senator and nodded.

"Good, sir, I'm glad I found you. We have big trouble. Curt just rode in from the north range, up where the Sweet Springs River runs near the Circle J. We got big troubles."

"Catch your breath, man," Senator Wallington said. "Are you sure this is important? We're right in the middle of setting up Penny's rescue."

"You'll want to know about this, Senator. Curt said that the river has dried up. Not a drop of water coming down. He followed up the dry bed until he found the problem. The Circle J has thrown up a dam across the river and diverted it into a ditch they dug so it runs down through the Circle J. Curt said it looked like an old river bottom and figured the Sweet Springs River might have gone that direction hundreds of years ago. The problem is it will run down all the way on Circle J land. Without that water our cattle will all die."

Senator Wallington sat down suddenly. "Why, that's illegal. You can't divert a natural river course. I can get a court order to blow up that dam."

"But, Senator . . ."

"No buts about it. I'll get into town right now. The circuit court judge should be through in a week or so."

"Senator, what the man is trying to tell you is that by then all of your cattle will be dead," Spur said. "Something has to be done right now—today, tonight."

Ed Hunt nodded. "He's damn right, Senator. Looks like the dam's been in for a day or more. Already the river is running dry a mile above the ranch house."

"Get together twenty riders," Senator Wallington said. "Ray Jordan isn't going to get away with this. Make sure every man has a rifle and his six-gun. We're riding up there as soon as you get the men ready."

"I'm going along, Senator," Spur said. "This is a violation of law, and it's in my jurisdiction. Oh, I think you should be taking along at least two cases of dynamite, fuse and detonators. That dam has to be opened up tonight or your cattle are in real trouble."

The ride to the dam was ten miles and took them just over two hours. They cantered for a while, then walked, then cantered again to make up time.

Curt led them and stopped them at a line of green trees around the river.

"We're about a quarter of a mile from the dam," he told Spur and the senator. "There's enough cover to stay in all the way up to the dam, but we'll have to leave the horses here."

"How many men you think he has on guard duty?" Spur asked.

"I'd guess three will be up all night watching it," Curt said. "If they went to all that work, they'll want to protect it."

Spur nodded. He had broken the two cases of dynamite up into 20 stick batches that the men carried in their saddlebags. Now he had them take their saddlebags off and put them over their shoulders. He had the fuse and detonating caps.

The senator turned to Spur. "I'd just as soon you lead this. I don't plan on getting into a shootout with these guys in the dark. After a time we wouldn't be sure who was shooting who. Did enough of that in the big war. First we look over the place and see what we can do."

Spur nodded and took the lead as the 22 men struck out upstream.

The streambed was almost dry here. After 100 yards, Spur stopped and motioned the men to be quiet and stay put. He went on ahead alone. He moved without a sound and came to within 20 feet of the log and earthen dam that had been thrown up across what once must have been a three or four foot falls. So they had a foundation to work with. He circled to the left and saw no one. When he came to the slight backup of water behind the dam, he paused and watched the far bank.

He saw the glow of a cigarette. Next he heard some whispered words. At least two of them. No chance to capture them. He saw the way the dam was constructed and nodded. The dam was made of vertical logs dug into the bedrock or ground and held in place with horizontal logs. The water came downstream, hit the logs and then swept to the left into what must be a dug channel over a small rise where the water ran down a different valley.

Clearly illegal and deadly to the cattle on the Bar-W. Spur had an idea for the solution. He let it germinate a moment; then he turned and slipped back the way he had come.

He told the men what he wanted them to do. He had ten men move with him up the creek and around the dam. The others moved where they could see the slight rise of the barrier and the position of the guards.

"Nobody shoot until you hear two quick pistol shots from me," he said. "Then I want each you to put two rounds over the heads of the guards. We don't want any bloodshed here or it could kick into a real range war. Nobody really wants that. Agreed, Senator?"

"Oh, yes. Nobody wins a range war, especially the men who get shot up and killed. We don't want that."

Spur nodded and left with his ten men. He went far to the side, out 50 yards from the stream so they wouldn't be heard or seen. They slid through the night like ghosts, and Spur placed them in a line spread out ten yards apart in a small arc. Then he took dynamite from four of the men. He carried the 40 sticks of powder upstream and searched until he found what he wanted.

He took three pieces of driftwood and tied them together to form a small raft. On top of it he placed a ready-made 20-stick dynamite bomb. He cast a piece of wood into the water and watched it float downstream. A nearly full moon helped him, and he counted off 30 seconds before the wood hit the logs. He cut one piece of burning fuse off at six inches and one at eight. He stuffed one end of the longer one in a dynamite cap and pushed the cap into the top stick of dynamite.

To be safe, Spur made a second bomb similar to

the first one. When he was done he tested them both in the backwater near him. Both floated and kept the powder out of the water.

Spur pushed both bombs with him, struck a match, shielded it with his body to light the longer fuse and set it drifting downstream. He did the same thing with the second bomb, and a moment later both moved downstream, bobbing slightly in the current.

Spur waded out of the water silently, then hurried so he would be in back of his line of riflemen. He counted in one-second units as he ran toward the rifles. He found one of the men and slid to the ground beside him.

"Twenty-eight, twenty-nine, thirty," Spur said. The cowboy looked at him in surprise.

"What the hell?" he asked.

"About time for a big bang," Spur said.

They could both see the dam in the soft moonlight. A second or so later the sky blossomed with an artificial sunburst accompanied by a cracking, smashing explosion as one of the 20-stick bombs went off. Spur, blinded for a moment by the brilliant flash of light, closed his eyes and then opened them. The upright logs of the dam were still in place. The bomb had gone off too early.

In the sudden stillness after the bomb he heard shots and wails of someone near the dam. One man there evidently fired a shot. Spur was glad it wasn't two shots. The men screamed at one another, but Spur couldn't make out what they said.

He hadn't counted, but he figured it was about time for the next bomb to blow. It did so before he could warn the cowboy beside him. This time he heard the same crackling roaring blast of dynamite, but at the same time he caught the sound of splintering wood and rushing water.

There were more screams from the guards. Spur stood to see better and could tell that the center of the log dam had been blasted open. He could hear the fall of the water dropping down the four feet back into its normal course.

He drew his six-gun and fired two shots into the sky. Almost at once the men near him blasted their two rounds over the guards. From below the dam came 20 more rounds.

When the sound of the rifle shots faded into the distance, Spur stood and cupped his hands around his mouth.

"You men on the riverbank. You Circle J guards. Your job is over. You have two minutes to get out of there or the next rounds of cross fire will cut you to pieces. This is Spur McCoy. I'm a United States Secret Service Agent. You men are in violation of the law. If you don't withdraw at once you'll be arrested and jailed. Sentences for this kind of felony conviction are three to five years in the state prison."

Spur waited. He could hear the men talking among themselves.

Then a voice called out. "Yes, sir, we understand. We was just doing what the boss told us to do. Didn't know he was violating any laws. We're riding out of here right now."

Spur waited for five minutes. He could hear two, then three, then more horses ride away. He waved his line of men forward, and they walked up to what was left of the dam.

"Senator, you can bring your men up now. Looks like it's all clear here."

Spur inspected the dam. It had been well-made with a lot of logs put into its construction. He figured where to put the next charge and made up the bomb, a ten-stick bundle. He wedged it between two of the main supports on the left side of the dam.

"Fire in the hole," Spur called. "All you men get back at least fifty yards. I'm going to set off another charge." He heard the men moving in the dark.

Spur hadn't seen the senator yet.

"Everyone clear?" he called. "Take cover."

He bent and lit the fuse, then walked away. "I put a two-foot fuse on it, so anyone close by has two minutes to get away from the dam." He walked off 50 yards and waited.

The explosion was softer this time, since it was contained and expended its energy by blasting the logs apart and out of place.

Spur checked his work. Half the dam was down and scattered on both sides of the stream. He set two more charges, moved the men back and blasted the rest of the dam into splintered logs and kindling wood.

He stood in the darkness, watching the water pour over the four-foot fall and work its way downstream. Senator Wallington came and stood by him.

"You do good work on blasting, Spur McCoy. I hope you can work this effectively with the Comanches."

"I hope so too, Senator. Mostly it depends on how much they want horses and how well their summer hunt is going. I hope they have run into a good-sized herd of buffalo up there in the breaks."

The men had gone downstream to bring up their horses. Being cowboys they felt naked without a piece of horseflesh within reaching distance.

Spur told them to settle down for the rest of the night. By then it was after three A.M. Spur wanted to check the remains of the dam in the daylight. Might take another blast or two to make sure the Circle J people didn't try to rebuild the dam.

It took Spur three more blasts after daylight

when he could see where the charges should be placed, blasting down the last of the vertical logs and disintegrating the cross pieces that had held them. Most of the shattered logs lay downstream, but a few were above.

Spur put six cowboys on each log upstream and had them attach their ropes to them and have their horses drag the logs out of the way.

Spur eyed the ditch that the Circle J men had dug to channel the water into the next valley. It hadn't been extensive. He buried four two-stick bombs along the 50 feet of it, and when the charges went off the ditch was filled in with dirt.

They had it all cleaned up by eight o'clock and headed back for the ranch.

Senator Wallington rode beside Spur as they walked their mounts.

"Good job, McCoy. I'll get a report off to the President." He frowned. "Now, about the other part of your job. You still think the best way is to go in and bargain for Penny? A straight trade of her for the horses?"

"That's the most valuable thing in the world to these warriors. They live to steal horses, and then they enjoy their wealth or trade them for things they want. Yes, a straight trade. Horses for Penny is the best way to go."

"I hope so, McCoy. God, how I hope that you're right. That's my only child out there, the only family I have. You've got to bring her back to me safe and sound!"

Chapter Seven

That afternoon the hands began rounding up enough horses for the trade. Horseflesh was suddenly in short supply at the ranch. The 50 that had been stolen were the best of the cow horses, and several of the men had been put to breaking new mounts and getting them ready for roundup in the fall.

Now they had to get more horses off the range and cull out the best ones to save. The rest were put in a temporary corral to hold the mounts bound for the Indians.

Senator Wallington dogged the riders all afternoon, but it was plain that there would be no chance to get the 50 horses that day.

Spur told the senator he had a few things to do in town and rode in about three o'clock. His first order was some clean clothes, and then he decided a bath might be a good idea as well. When he was presentable, he had a leisurely early supper in the hotel dining room. He was almost through when he looked up and saw Tory Roth walking toward his table.

He stood and offered her a chair. She accepted it and ordered a cup of coffee. She watched him as he finished his supper. She had already eaten, she told him. When he was nearly done, she stared at him across the top of her coffee cup and a small frown edged onto her pretty face.

"Spur McCoy, I need you to help me with a serious matter."

Spur looked up at her, surprised at the tone of her voice.

"Anything I can do. I do have a small job starting tomorrow for a few days, but after that . . ."

"Oh, dear, I was hoping it might be sooner." Her hand under the table found his knee and worked higher.

"You see, I have this strange itching sensation in the most private place, and you're the only one who can scratch it the correct way." She smiled, her brown hair did a little dance around her face, and her brown eyes glistened. Her hand made it to his crotch. No one else could see this bit of public display. Spur sat there watching her.

She rubbed his crotch, searching for a hardness. It didn't come.

"You think this problem of yours might wait until later tonight. Say about eight o'clock in my room?"

"I think it might wait that long." She pulled her hand away with a small sigh, then stood. "Thank you, Mr. McCoy, for the coffee. I appreciate it."

She turned and walked away. Spur marveled at the way her tight little buns bounced and rolled under the dress she wore. Spur watched her walk out of sight and called for another cup of coffee. When it was gone he paid his tab and left.

He walked down the street to the sheriff's office.

The time was shortly after seven, and Sheriff Ben Johnson was still working at his desk.

"Got time for a beer?" Spur asked, marching in through the front door.

Ben turned, wiped at his eyes and nodded. "Damn, sounds good. I've had nothing but headaches all day. The paperwork end of this job is getting bigger and bigger all the time. I remember when we just threw paper in the fire to get it started on a cold morning."

Spur laughed. He had to do something to cover up his surprise every time he saw Ben. The man was not a tenth of the lawman he used to be. Ben stood and looked at the gunbelt hanging on a peg by the door. He shrugged and lifted it off the hook.

"Don't wear it, Ben," Spur said. "Damned fine way to get yourself killed."

"Probably, but then there don't seem to be much of a good way to let go of what once was. Hell, you're getting older yourself there, McCoy."

Spur shrugged. "I can't argue with that. You had supper yet?"

"Don't eat a whole lot anymore. Just don't seem to need it. Have breakfast and then a sandwich or something along in the afternoon." Ben straightened up a little from the stooped way he had been walking.

"You trying to wet-nurse me here, youngster?"

Spur laughed. "I tried a wet nurse once. She was nothing special but that breast milk is a real treat. Tastes better than I ever imagined."

"You're impossible, McCoy. Let's have a beer and tell lies about Colorado. Remember Colorado? Hell, that was a great place to be back in the late sixties. Not a shadow of a lawman in most out of the way places. I was town marshall in three towns all at once. I'd go from one to the other."

They laughed their way into the next saloon that came along, the Hangman's Roost. It was only a couple of notches up from a barrel bar. It had a wooden floor, a real bar with a foot rail and all, and a dozen tables for card games. Along the sides they had built in booths where the drinkers could partly hide themselves.

The house got nothing from the card games, so they had two chippies who pestered the players for drinks every five minutes.

Spur bought two draft beers at the bar, and he and Ben took a back table so they could watch the action. They were halfway through Colorado, having ticked off six different towns where Ben had plied his lawman's trade, when a young man walked into the bar and bellowed something as loud as he could.

All conversation stopped. The kid wasn't over 22 or 23, Spur figured. He was six feet tall and Texas-slim, with dangling arms and a brand-new white, high-crowned Stetson. Spur knew the kid was trouble.

"Hey, assholes, can't nobody hear in this pigpen, or don't any of you understand English? I asked if Sheriff Johnson is in here."

Spur stood up and walked toward the young man, who had a holster tied low on his leg and a hogleg showing out of the leather.

"I said, is the damn Sheriff Johnson in here?"

"Who the hell is asking?" Spur bellowed back at him, just as loud and with a snarl in it that brought an immediate reaction from the kid.

"I did, Sonny Boone—and you best remember that name, if you live long enough. You Sheriff Johnson?"

"I didn't say. Usually I mop up the outhouse with scum like you. Why do you want to see the sheriff?"

"I got some legal problems for him. Fact of the matter is he should be a dead man. You Sheriff Ben Johnson?"

"I'm Sheriff Johnson, son," Ben said, coming up beside Spur. "Your mother know you're carrying a dangerous weapon like that? Usually we don't allow young boys to pack a pistol in this town. You said you wanted to see me?"

The tone of Ben's words had been as cold as winter ice, as chilling as a summer's dip in a glacier-fed mountain stream. The one who called himself Boone took a step backward.

His surly expression vanished, and when he stared at Ben, his mouth gaped open, surprise bathing his face. He frowned, then rubbed his face with one big hand.

"Are you . . . ?" He stopped. "You the same Ben Johnson who did Little Bill Elliott over in Sage couple of years ago?"

"I worked Sage. I don't keep track of the no-account slime I have to put down. Why do you ask?" The same dead-level tone with icicles all over it came from Ben. His eyes stared at the bigger man, and for just a moment there was some hesitation by the man who called himself Boone.

That was what Ben had been waiting for. He struck like a half-starved rattlesnake who had surprised a desert rat.

"Son, if you got no business in this establishment or in Sweet Springs, I'd advise you to be on your mount and ride out of town. We don't much hold with gunfighters in this town."

Sonny Boone gulped. He took half a step backward; then he nodded. "Yes, sir, Mr. Johnson. I rightly think that I can do that. Just passing through. Stay the night and I'll be gone with sunup."

"Good. I'll be checking on you. You best be

moving out of here, Boone, and stop disturbing the patrons."

Boone said nothing, bobbed his head, took two steps backward, then turned and hurried out the saloon door. When the door slammed behind him, a small cheer went up, then a larger one. Ben went back to the table and his mug of beer. Before he could reach for it, the barkeep hurried over with two fresh brews for the sheriff and his friend.

"Thanks, Ben, for getting rid of that trash," the apron said. "Compliments of the house." He hurried back to the bar, where the talk was how Ben had stared down another young gun.

Ben sipped the brew and shook his head. "That's three times this summer, Spur. I don't know how much longer I can bluff these young bloods. One of these days one won't be awed at all. He'll just keep boring in and boring in and I'll have to show my hand."

"Stop wearing the gun," Spur said.

Ben scowled. "Spur, you know I can't do that. People in town will start to talk, and then the word will spread on the prairie telegraph. There'd be ten guns in town within a week, all with me as the target."

"Maybe, maybe not. There's always Chicago."

They finished their beers, and right on schedule the barkeep brought over two more. Spur paid for these, tossing the man 20 cents. When the apron left with the empty mugs, Spur shook his head.

"Damn expensive town you've got here, Sheriff. When did beer go from a nickel to a dime?"

"Day I hired in. That's what pays my salary."

They chuckled about it a minute, then were back talking about Colorado, evidently the best time of life for Ben Johnson.

At eight-thirty, Spur said he had an early morning

and told the old lawman good-bye. "Still think you should hang up that six-gun in the closet and forget where it is," Spur said.

"Hell, I could also change my name. Who would recognize me? I saw how surprised you were when I turned around in the office that first day." Ben sighed. "Hell, get out of here and go find yourself a good woman and get married and turn in your badge and get an honest job, like shoveling shit out of a livery somewhere. Do something that will help people."

Spur held out his hand, shook the feeble grip and left the saloon with a catch in his throat. He had a feeling that Ben was setting himself up to be killed by some hot young blood eager to make a name with his Colt .45.

Spur walked up to his second-floor room in the hotel. He didn't bother to knock. He figured that the door was unlocked and that Tory would be inside. He stood to the side of the door, as he always did, and turned the knob. Unlocked. He pushed it in hard so it hit the wall. The lamp was lit inside. He looked around the jamb and grinned.

"About time you got here," Tory said.

Spur went in and closed the door.

"I'd like to make a deposit," he said.

Tory sat on the bed and grinned up at him. She wore a bright red dress that brought out some red tints in her soft brown hair. The dress pushed up her breasts, and she had unbuttoned it halfway down to show a long line of cleavage.

"I'd much rather you made two deposits. I have three windows open."

Spur sat down beside her, and she stroked his inner thigh. "You look worried, McCoy."

"I am. You know the sheriff?"

"Sure, Ben Johnson. He's a famous gunfighter.

77

Cleaned up half the towns in the west."

"Now he can't even hold a gun. When the word gets out there's going to be half a dozen young punks a day coming to town to test Ben and try to kill him."

"Why, for goodness sakes?"

"To make a reputation for themselves. So they can say, 'I'm the guy who outdrew the famous Ben Johnson. Beat him and killed him down in Texas'."

"They'd do that to an old man?"

"Just as soon as they pick up the scent."

She unbuttoned the rest of the fasteners over her breasts and pushed one of his hands in the opening. His fingers closed around her bare breast.

"Oh, damn, Tory. Why do I love tits so much? I really get excited when I see a great pair, or when I touch one no matter how big or little it is."

"Make love to me there," Tory said. "I'll hold them together, and we'll use some lotion I have. Let's try it."

Spur stared at her, then helped her lift the red dress over her head. She wore only short, tight silk panties under the dress. She went on her knees and brought her breasts up to Spur's face.

"My little girl titties do want you to fuck them, Spur McCoy. They get left out of the good part. They really want you, Spur. Please do them."

Spur chuckled. "Never had tits talk to me before or give me such a passionate plea. First you have to undress me."

She did.

A minute later Spur hovered over her, and he pushed his whanger between her breasts where she held them together. She lay on her back and grinned.

"This is absolutely wild, Spur. I never have done anything so strange and wonderful before. Come on, do it. I want to watch your big prick spurt all over my titties."

Spur laughed and started to pump. He was surprised how easy it was and how well it worked. He had tried it once before, but it had never actually happened. The other girl's breasts had been too small, he had decided.

Tory increased pressure on him when she held her breasts tighter together, and he sensed his own excitement building.

"Oh, yes, you're starting to react," Tory yelped. "You're breathing faster. I've never really listened to you and watched you before when you're fucking. Hey, you're working harder, poking me better. Yes, Spur. Go, go, go!"

He decided it was her reaction almost as much as his, but a few strokes later he was over the top and slamming down the far side, shooting off all over her.

Then he fired again, emptied his magazine and eased off of her.

"That was just fantastic. I saw you shoot each load. It was great. That's what goes on inside! Oh, I'll love you forever for doing my titties that way. Now, let me get cleaned up a little. Then when you have a rest we'll see how much of a fine time we can have tonight. I do hope you won't have to get up early in the morning. Nothing starts off the day so good as a little morning lovemaking. Don't you agree?"

Spur said something that sounded like yes and turned to look at her. She had moved to the washstand and was cleaning off her breasts. He watched, fascinated. For a minute he wanted to go help, but he watched and grinned when she looked over at him.

"Oh, good, you're still alive. You still haven't made

that deposit we talked about. I think five deposits would be about right. That way I'll be pleasantly sore tomorrow and wonder if I'm pregnant, but I know I won't be because I finished my bleeding just four days ago and that's too fast for any of those little ova to be swimming around.

"Oh, yes, I know all about the reproductive cycle of the human being. It's natural and simple and can happen quite easily if the woman is at the right stage of ovulation. That's why I'm always careful, but I'm not sure now if I was the sterile one or if my ex-husband was. If I do ever get pregnant I'll be sure to tell him about it and make sure he knows that he only fires blanks from that little prick of his."

She grinned. "You must think I'm awful, but lots of times I talk up a storm when I get fucked good. You ready yet? Come on, let's give it a try. I'll even let you be on top the first time. You still didn't tell me if you have an early rising tomorrow."

"No early call. We'll have plenty of time for some soft, gentle lovemaking after the sun comes up and before you need to go to the bank."

"Don't talk about work. I hate it. I have to be a teller for a whole year before I get to take over the loan department. That will be ever so much more interesting."

She sat down beside him on the bed in her naked splendor. "The girls are all clean, see?"

She hung one large firm breast over where he lay on his back, and he reached up and kissed it.

"Oh, yes, I think this is going to be a fine night and morning of lovemaking."

It was.

Chapter Eight

Spur McCoy rode into the Bar-W Ranch about eight the next morning and met an unhappy senator in the ranch house kitchen.

"Those damn Comanches stole the best riding stock I had. Now we're trying to get a remuda together for the fall roundup and at the same time come up with thirty-five mounts for you to drive north for Penny.

"They stole over fifty head, and now I'm bleeding out another thirty-five. Damn! I'm not begrudging the mounts for Penny. I just wish I had enough to do what I need to do."

"How much time do you need?" Spur asked.

"Another four or five days. The boys have spotted a herd of wild mustangs about a day's ride out. They'll go catch as many of them as they can. Thirty-five, you say?"

"Maybe more. Depends how good a bargainer the boss warrior up there is." Spur scowled. "Four or five

81

days, you say. That changes things. I don't think it's a good idea to let Penny sit up there that much more time without some hope. Captives like Penny can get frantic after a while."

"So what can we do? Send her a telegram?"

"Might be able to, at that. Only I'd have to deliver it. Worth thinking about for me to slip into camp, surprise them and then try to bargain, instead of simply waltzing up there with a herd of mustangs."

"Walk into their camp? Wouldn't they cut you to pieces before they found out what you wanted?"

"They'd try. What I'd have to do would be to surprise them somehow, impress them that I was as good an Indian, as good a fighter and horseman as they were. Gain some respect."

"If they didn't kill you first."

"Always a problem. I bleed just as fast as anybody else."

"So why risk it?"

"Asked myself that same question a dozen times. Turns out this is my job. I have to think what's best for the victim here, and that's Penny."

Senator Wallington nodded and paced the kitchen. "She was an innocent. Never even been out on a social occasion with a boy. I mean she was a virgin. I don't expect we'll find her that way when we get her back."

"Probably not. If the warrior who captured her keeps her as a wife, then he probably will have taken her by this time. That would be the best we could hope for."

"Damn! I knew I shouldn't have let her come home to be with that damn mare. Foal or no foal, she should have been in Washington and safe."

"Easy to figure that looking backward," Spur said and stood. "Hell, I guess I should get a horse from you and some food and a pot or two and a couple of blankets and go for a ride."

"To the Comanche camp?"

"About the only thing left to do. Get those horses together fast as you can. Have at least fifty you can spare, maybe sixty-five. Some of these Comanches can be tough traders."

The senator watched him. "I'll get them somehow. She's my daughter, my only child. We'll do it. We have to."

Two days later, Spur McCoy edged closer to the edge of a thick spot of brush and watched the Comanche camp 500 yards ahead. He had seen half a dozen hunters moving through the wooded valley. It was as close as he wanted to get. He had left his horse, camping gear and food two miles back in heavy brush. There was only a small chance any of the hunters would stumble onto his horse.

He waited. The activity around the camp seemed normal. He could make out women working on skins, warriors riding here and there on their war ponies. He saw young boys playing with their small bows and practicing with their arrows.

He had two hours to wait for darkness, then six more hours before it would be late enough and the camp asleep before he did what he felt he must.

Spur dozed.

He came awake with a start. Someone was close by. He looked around first without moving his head. No one. He checked cautiously to his right. There, not 20 feet from him, stood a Comanche hunter, bow and arrow poised. He looked straight ahead, away from Spur.

The Comanche concentrated on the spot, then slowly drew the arrow back all the way, waited a few seconds, then released it. It flew straight ahead and hit a rabbit, skewering it through the shoulders. The hunter ran forward, dispatched the small animal, hung it on a rawhide leather strip over his back and moved off into the brush.

Spur let out a long-held breath. Too close. He heard two more hunters before dusk at last settled down and the woods quieted. An owl hooted; then a bird called from far away, and there was an answering call.

Spur stretched and left from his hideout. He walked around for a few minutes to get his legs working again, then worked his way through the brush and trees without making a sound along the side of the creek that ran from the Comanche camp.

He stayed well back of the water and on the far side from most of the tepees. Slowly he moved on until he was 50 yards from the first Comanche tepee.

He checked to see where the largest one was. Farther along. He moved again and came out about 30 yards from the big tepee with the flying eagle painted on the side.

That was his objective. He hadn't figured out the best way to surprise the savages, but he had to show them something that was out of the ordinary, something they wouldn't expect a mere white man to do.

But not yet. It had to be just at sunrise or shortly afterward. He had no weapons. He had left his six-gun, the Spencer rifle and even his boot knife back with the horse and supplies. He hadn't come here to fight the whole Comanche band. They would see that at once. A white man in an Indian camp of his own free will and without weapons would impress them.

Maybe if he took off his shirt? No. He needed

something dramatic. At last he thought of it. It should work. He settled down. Nothing to do now but catch a nap until dawn came.

He awoke twice during the night, both times when one of the dogs in the camp barked a welcome to the moon. For a moment he wondered where the Indians got their dogs. They had them long before the white invaders had come and they used them as beasts of burden.

When the Indians first saw the horse the Spaniards introduced to the plains, the Indians called them Seven-Dog, because they could carry as much as seven dogs.

His mind wandered for a moment; then he gave a big sigh and went back to sleep.

A half hour before dawn, he awoke again. This time he stood quickly and scanned the camp. No one had moved yet. There were no guards or lookouts. He walked quietly into the camp, around to the front of the head man's tepee and found a level place near the entrance flap.

He sat down, crossed his legs and folded his arms. That would be a big enough shock for the Comanches. To think that a white man had stolen into their camp without their knowing it and calmly sat down outside the tepee owned by the chief and waited for him to come out would amaze them.

Spur guessed that others would see him first. Would they sound an alarm, or would they rush up and challenge him to battle? Maybe they would simply run him through with a lance, but Spur didn't think so.

They would be angry, but also a bit awed by his bravery and his nerve. It wouldn't be long.

Spur heard mutterings inside the tepee beside him, but no one came out.

Across the way two warriors left their shelters,

stretched and went into the brush to relieve themselves. Spur waited. An old woman left a tepee next to the big one, but she turned the other way and didn't see him.

A moment later a warrior emerged from the same tepee. He turned toward Spur and stopped as if he had seen a huge bear charging down on him. The Indian stared at Spur for a moment; then he bellowed a way cry and charged toward Spur. The warrior had no weapon with him.

He sprinted the 20 yards and stopped just as a tall Indian came out of the leader's shelter. Spur had sat so he was half facing the tepee's flap. He stared hard at the big Indian, who wore only his breechclout. Spur figured he was five-ten, tall for a Comanche.

The first warrior who saw Spur bellowed something, but the leader made a curt gesture with his hand. He jabbered something to the other man, then turned to Spur. He said three words that Spur didn't understand.

Spur stood slowly, faced the big Indian and gave the Plains sign language for friend. He held up his right hand, bent the last two fingers to his palm and held them with his thumb.

The cry of the first warrior had tumbled two dozen warriors from their sleep. Now they circled Spur and the leader, all with at least one weapon.

The tall man made a sign back at Spur.

The Indian held his hand flat in front of him with the back up and fingers pointing to the left. He swung the hand to the right and front with the palm up. He repeated the sign twice.

"No?" Spur said. "English? Anyone speak English?"

One of the warriors charged Spur, hit him with his shoulder and knocked him into the dirt.

The leader barked out a command, and the

warrior scowled and edged back into the throng. Spur stood, never even looking at the Indian who had knocked him down.

He made the friend sign again and showed that he had no weapons. Spur made the motion as if drawing a six-gun and shooting, then made the sign for "no" and looked at the leader.

The Indian scowled and said something to the crowd. A few of them relaxed and walked away. Most watched.

Spur reached back into the past and came up with the remembered signs that he needed. He asked the obvious leader of the band where Flying Eagle was.

The leader promptly signed back that Flying Eagle was a spirit now, gone to the big sky.

The man waved the others away, then sat and motioned for Spur to sit as well.

"Wantabe," the Indian said.

Spur repeated the word. The big Indian pointed to his chest and said the name again.

"Spur," McCoy said, pointing to his own chest and saying the name again.

Slowly they communicated in sign language.

"You surprised us," Wantabe said.

"You were not expecting visitors," Spur signed back.

"You long way from other *tosi tivo*."

"White men go many places."

"You, Spur, shamed whole camp by slipping in like the north wind when no one watched," Wantabe signed.

"No shame. Spur half-Comanche."

Wantabe frowned. "You ride, you throw knife, shoot bow?"

Spur smiled and nodded.

"I come looking for *yo-oh hobt pa-pi*. The yellow-hair girl."

Wantabe said nothing and stared at Spur without a sound. Most of the other warriors and curious women had left. The two sat alone.

"You have the yellow hair?" Spur signed.

"All Indians have black hair."

"The *tosi-tivo*," Spur said. He signed for girl, then said *tosi-tivo* again.

"*No bueno* you *está*," Wantabe said.

Spur reacted to the Spanish. He had forgotten that most of the Comanches used a lot of Spanish in their trips as they rode back and forth across the border.

They spoke quicker in Spanish, even though Spur's was spotty.

"I'm here to talk about the white girl, the yellow-haired one."

Wantabe looked away. "You shamed my clan. You slipped in our midst like a spirit. You are a brave warrior, but can you fight?"

"I fight when I must. More is gained by talking than fighting."

"A contest. Can you throw a knife?"

"I've pitched one a time or two."

Wantabe turned and shouted to a warrior who stood nearby with all of his weapons. The warrior was nearly six feet tall, a giant of a man for a Comanche.

"You will have a contest with our most powerful warrior, Sitting Squirrel."

"Throwing knives at a target?"

Wantabe nodded.

Five minutes later the men stood at a line in the dirt. Twenty feet away grew a cottonwood tree, feeding from the stream.

Against the trunk, six leaves had been fastened with small wooden slivers. The leaves were an inch wide and two inches long.

A woman brought out a blanket and laid it on the ground. It held a dozen knives of several types.

"Choose three knives," Wantabe said.

Spur squatted in front of the blanket and hefted one knife. The handle was far too heavy. He tested several more, then picked out three that were about the same weight, length and balance.

Sitting Squirrel selected three knives from those remaining.

They gave Spur the first throw.

"Throw one knife, hit one leaf. Then Sitting Squirrel throws one."

Spur checked the knife again. He had never been the best at throwing a knife. Trying these without some practice might be a disaster.

He stepped up to the line, held the knife by the side of the blade and threw. The knife made one complete turn and drove into the tree but missed one of the leaves by an inch.

Sitting Squirrel grinned, went to the line and drove his knife through one of the leaves.

Spur took his turn again, this time slicing into one leaf from the side. Wantabe held up one finger on each hand. Even so far. Sitting Squirrel threw his second knife and sliced into a leaf.

Spur took his last throw. He chose the leaf on the left side of the tree. There was one three inches directly below it. If he got the alignment right he had a chance of hitting either one. He threw at the top one. The blade cut squarely in the center of the lower leaf. Tied—two, two.

Sitting Squirrel strode to the line. It was his game to win or tie. He took his time, aimed and threw. His blade missed the leaf by the width of a bowstring. Sitting Squirrel ran to the tree and checked the blade. No part of the steel touched the leaf.

"Tie," Spur said.

"Ride," Wantabe said.

Spur held up his hand. "Sitting Squirrel must ride someone else's horse. He can't ride his own war pony. He must ride one of your mounts."

Wantabe nodded. "Fair," he said.

Both men were brought Indian ponies. Spur sat barebacked on his mount and touched it with his heels, and it pranced away. He used the hackamore to guide the animal and realized in a flash that the horse had been knee and thigh and heel trained. It took its commands and directions from pressure of the rider's legs and feet. He wasn't sure he could make it do what he wanted it to with the hackamore bridle.

He kept his feet and legs as motionless as possible. Riding without a saddle and the familiar stirrups was much different. They were each given a short period of time to get used to their mounts. Then Wantabe bellowed, and they both rode back to the flat, open meadow well below the camp itself.

Now he noted that the mount had a four-inch wide surcingle around its belly and back. He'd seen Indians use the belt-like device to hold on to as they did various feats on horseback. He'd never tried anything fancy like that.

This time Sitting Squirrel went first. He rode out 30 feet and dropped a small basket on the ground. The warrior rode back, turned and galloped toward the basket. At the last moment he bent low off the horse, holding the surcingle, balanced, reached almost to the ground, snatched up the basket and rode back to the others.

Spur frowned.

"You do," Wantabe said in Spanish.

A young boy ran the basket out to the same place from which the other rider had retrieved it. Spur judged the distance, took a firm grip on the surcingle and rode.

He bent low, felt himself slipping and jolted back on the mount, but by that time the horse was past the basket.

Wantabe kept score. The riding contest went on all afternoon, and by the time Wantabe called it to a halt, Sitting Squirrel was ahead 14 to 6.

They walked back to the tepees and Wantabe motioned to Spur to sit down outside his shelter.

"You damn good for white man," he said in Spanish.

"Thanks. Now, can we talk about Penny, the yellow hair?"

Wantabe shook his head. "Tomorrow, after next contest."

Before Spur could ask what it would be, two Indian women brought out large bowls of stew and slabs of roasted meat. Spur bit into it and recognized the wild taste of antelope. Yes, he'd heard there were still herds of them in this part of Texas.

Spur ate his fill. His bowl wasn't yet empty of the thin stew, and he knew it would be an insult not to finish it. He gulped down the last of the food and leaned back.

"Rest well, white man Spur," Wantabe said in Spanish. "Tomorrow is the last contest, the fight of the knife and rawhide."

Spur looked puzzled for a moment, unsure of what the Comanche was talking about; then he remembered. It was a knife fight in which both men held one end of a three-foot-long piece of rawhide by their teeth. To drop the end of rawhide was to forfeit the fight and your life. It was a battle to the death! And if Spur didn't win, Penny would lose any hope of ever being saved.

Chapter Nine

Spur watched the Indian clan leader. He was serious about the knife fight to the death. They had been toying with him. Wantabe stood, and Spur rose as well.

"Now, Spur, we see if you really are half-Comanche."

Spur nodded without changing his expression and walked directly into the brush behind Wantabe's tepee. He would find a place where he could cover himself with some leaves or tree boughs and try to get some sleep.

He would need it.

He had only seen one such fight. Not even the Indians held them often. It was a kind of death sentence for one of the two men. Sometimes it was used to settle a rage between two warriors that could not be satisfied any other way.

Spur had never heard of it being used with a white man.

He had little sleep that night. Somehow he had to figure out a way to stay alive. If that meant killing or badly wounding this large Indian, so be it. Him or me. He hadn't heard that kind of life or death reasoning since the war.

Tomorrow morning he indeed would be in a war, a war for his very life. He could use a knife, but the Comanche warriors had practiced using a blade since they were four years old. How could he match up against that?

He figured his only hope was to make it a quick fight. If it came down to endurance, the younger warrior would be able to outlast him and wear him out—and kill him.

Spur dismissed that option at once. He would live. Just how, right now, he wasn't certain. Make the Indian always face the sun? That would help. Take a damaging cut to his arm to permit him to make a killing thrust? Maybe. He was sure that Sitting Squirrel knew all of the tricks. He would be ready for them. What wouldn't he be ready for?

Spur could think of nothing.

He tried to sleep. Two or three times he dozed off only to awake with a dream of a huge knife about to slice him in half. Every little sound seemed to become amplified a hundred times. The barking dogs were the worst. Even an owl hooting 100 yards or more away ruined any chance for sleep.

Every idea he came up with split apart at the seams. He could slip away in the night and get to his horse and probably get away from a Comanche search party. But then he would never be able to bargain for Penny.

He hadn't seen her but felt that she was close by. They were hiding her. He had asked one small boy about the yellow hair. The boy only laughed and ran away.

When morning came, he washed his face and arms in the cold stream and drank his fill. He didn't want anything to eat this morning. It would only slow him down.

He went through a series of stretching exercises to get his muscles ready; then he walked up to Wantabe's big tepee and waited. A half hour later Sitting Squirrel walked up and sat down on the other side of the front of the tepee.

Two hours after sunrise, Wantabe came out and nodded at the two contestants. They walked to the cleared place around the council fire, and Wantabe unwrapped the length of rawhide from his waist. It had been cut on each end, and a heavy knot had been tied there to give the men something to hold on to with their teeth.

Spur heard a baby cry, and when he looked around for the first time, he noticed that at least half of the camp had gathered around the circle that had been drawn on the ground. The surrounding people provided two services. They clearly outlined the space for the fight, and they kept either man from running away.

A woman came out with a buffalo robe and unrolled it. Inside were six knives, all of the same length. Some had blades that would cut either way.

Sitting Squirrel went to the blanket, picked out a knife and stood with it to the side. Spur looked at the blades and shook his head. He turned to Wantabe.

"This is not a civilized method of settling an argument," he said in broken, incomplete Spanish. "I refuse to fight this man."

Wantabe lifted his brows. "It is the way of the people. If you don't fight, he will kill you before you can take a dozen steps. If you fight, you might kill him. It is your choice."

Spur followed most of the Spanish and understood. If he didn't fight he was a dead man. Him or me. Spur went to the blanket and picked a knife that was the heaviest, most sturdily built. It had a one-way cutting blade, but it was thick and strong.

The Indian woman wrapped up the buffalo robe and faded back into the crowd. Spur guessed there must be well over 100 men, women and children watching.

Wantabe turned to the people, held up one arm and spoke to them in quick, short sentences. Then he turned to Spur.

"I told them you are a ghost who swept into our camp like a spirit. Now you must prove you are worthy of our trust. Now we have the knife and rawhide fight."

Again the Spanish was rough, and Spur's understanding even rougher, but he caught the idea. One way or the other blood would flow.

Spur took off his heavy shirt and his undershirt and stood bare to the waist. The Indian wore only his breechclout and was barefoot. Spur considered that. Yes! It could be a chance. It would be a total surprise and shock to the big Indian. Spur still wore his solid cowboy boots with big heels and hard leather toes.

If he had a chance, he would kick the Indian. He'd seen a kick boxer once from the Far East who used his feet more than his fists. He didn't have the restraint of the rawhide and had spun and jumped and kicked. He had knocked out his opponent in less than a minute.

Spur considered it again. Yes, it was a way out. There was nothing said about any rules or methods of fighting. Eye gouging, ear tearing, ball kicking would all be legal. What could they say once their man was down and dead.

Wantabe approached him and motioned. A line

had been drawn in the center of the circle. The contestants put a foot or boot at the line. Then Wantabe handed one end of the rawhide to Spur and the other end to Sitting Squirrel. Both put the rawhide in their mouths and clamped down teeth. The rawhide tasted awful, but Spur knew that was the least of his problems.

Wantabe now pushed each man back until the rawhide was taut. He looked at both men, then took three steps away and held up his right fist. Wantabe brought his arm down and shouted, *"Hirah!"* The fight began.

Sitting Squirrel circled slowly to the left, then feinted to the right and drove in with his blade aimed at Spur's knife arm. Spur threw up his left arm and swung his own blade like a saber. It missed. He held the knife as he would a saber, not like a stabbing knife. With the blade pointing forward from his fist, he could slash either way or stab forward.

Sitting Squirrel held his blade the same way. Spur knew this must be a fast fight; otherwise he was breakfast for the buzzards. He feinted one way, jogged back, then feinted again and carried through with a swinging swipe at Sitting Squirrel's knife arm. The tip of the blade scratched a blood line across the thick arm but hurt the warrior little.

A shout went up from the watchers.

Sitting Squirrel looked in surprise at Spur. He stood with his legs wide, dancing on his toes to be ready for the next thrust.

Spur followed with a straight thrust forward that drove the Indian back a step. He kept his feet wide for balance.

Now, Spur decided. He was moving forward, took a half-step with his left foot, then swung his right foot up in a vicious kick as hard as he could.

He saw the surprise in the Indian's eyes. The warrior tried to protect his crotch, but his legs were set too wide. Spur's heavy boot slanted off the Indian's left leg and drove upward. He felt the heavy toe of his boot ram into the soft breechclout and into Sitting Squirrel's scrotum.

The force of the kick smashed both Sitting Squirrel's testicles against his pelvic bones, bringing a great scream of pain from the large Indian. He dropped the rawhide from his mouth, let the knife fall from his hand and crumpled to the ground where he curled into a fetal ball, screaming in pain from his crushed testicles.

Spur reached for the other man's blade and drove it deeply into the ground. Then he stood over the fallen warrior and placed his knife against the screaming man's throat.

The Comanches around the circle were riveted. No one moved. No one spoke. All eyes watched Spur as he drew a thin blood line, barely breaking the skin of the Indian warrior. Then he put his knife down with the tip of it on a rock and jammed his boot down against the blade. The steel snapped in half. Spur picked up the halves of the knife and threw then into the stream.

He pointed to Sitting Squirrel. "Here is a mighty warrior who does not deserve to die," Spur said in his inadequate Spanish. "There will be no widow in his tepee tonight. He will live to help his people in their long struggle for survival. This act of rewarding a brave warrior with his life is the way of my people."

Wantabe stepped into the fighting circle. He held up his hand for quiet and quickly translated what Spur had said for those not understanding Spanish.

A large cheer went up, and people crowded into

the ring to touch Spur and to smile and wave at him.

Spur wasn't sure what to do. He stood there nodding and smiling. At last he reached for his shirt and put it on, tucking the tails in his pants. Two men came and carried Sitting Squirrel away; he still couldn't walk.

Spur motioned to the injured man. "He'll heal in time and have many children," Spur said to Wantabe in his poor Spanish. The Comanche leader stared hard at Spur, then gave one nod.

"He lost. He should have died."

Spur shook his head. "Sitting Squirrel is a good warrior. He'll recover and do great things for the Comanche."

Most of the spectators had drifted away. Spur turned to the leader. "It is after the contest. Now we will talk about the yellow hair, Penny."

Wantabe motioned for Spur to follow him, and they walked back and sat outside the leader's tepee.

Wantabe looked at Spur to start the talk.

"Is Penny well and safe?" he asked, using Spanish again.

"Yes. In my care."

"Penny is the daughter of one of the big chiefs in Washington, D.C. He sits in the high council. He can command the army. This big chief could send a thousand warriors to surround the Comanche camp."

"If so, Penuu die when blue legs fire first shot."

"I know that. I told the big chief. He has not sent for the army. He is willing to trade for Penny."

There was no change in the expression of the Indian leader.

"Penuu is third wife of Wantabe. Why would I want to trade her?"

"If army comes, Penny will die, but so will half of your warriors. Your band will be crushed. You will have to steal away and beg to join another band of Comanches where you will be only another warrior."

"I think of this."

"No need to bring in the horse soldiers, if you trade for Penny."

Wantabe picked up a stick off the ground and began to draw in the sand in front of him. He did not look at Spur. He simply drew designs and rubbed them out and drew more. Sometimes he looked away at the small stream and the young boys playing naked in the water.

Spur wished he had a watch he could check. The time stretched out. It was a waiting game, and Spur was as good at it as the Indian. After 20 minutes of no response, Wantabe turned and looked at Spur. There was a touch of respect in his face and his voice.

"Wantabe trade Penuu for ten times ten rifles and ten times ten bullets for each weapon."

This time it was Spur who did the silent treatment, not responding. He looked away at the river, then closed his eyes and practiced his deep breathing. After what he figured was ten long minutes he shook his head.

"The white man has laws preventing selling or trading to the Comanche any firearms. To do so would make the big chief Wallington a criminal, and he would go to prison. He would rather see his daughter die than to break the laws that he has helped make in Washington."

The younger, pregnant woman, evidently wife number one or two of Wantabe, came out the tepee flap and said something. Wantabe nodded and turned to Spur.

"Come, eat."

To Spur's surprise the Indian led the way inside the tepee. The sudden gloom stopped Spur for a moment. Even the light, coming through the smoke hole on top and around the sides where the covering had been rolled up, left the interior of the tepee so smoky and dim that he could barely see.

Spur let his eyes adjust, then moved to the spot Wantabe motioned to and sat down. As he did he heard a shriek from the other side of the fire. A moment later the pregnant wife led Penny around the fire and left her in front of Spur, who stood up.

She wore her fine doeskin dress with beadwork, and her hair had been loosened from the braids and hung around her shoulders and down her back in a long, curly blonde shower.

"Penny Wallington?" Spur asked.

She nodded. He saw how her face worked, and he knew that she didn't trust herself to speak.

"Wantabe and I have been talking about your coming back to the ranch. We have to do much more talking, but we'll work out some kind of a trade. Are you well?"

She nodded.

"Have you been treated well?"

Again she nodded.

"Has Wantabe taken you as his third wife?"

Tears spilled down her cheeks this time. "Yes," she said, her voice quavering.

"Penny, you may be here another week before we work this all out, but we will get you out of here."

"I thought you were going to be killed today," Penny said. "I saw the fight. You were brave letting the warrior live."

"I'm not a savage. Take heart and bear up. I'll have you free just as soon as I can."

She sat down beyond the other two wives, and they all ate. There was more of the roasted antelope and fresh-picked berries and some kind of stew with wild onions in it. The Comanches may have traded horses for the onions, Spur figured.

When the food was gone, Wantabe motioned to Spur, and they stood and left the tepee. Spur had one last glance at Penny, nodding and giving her a big smile.

Outside Wantabe motioned for Spur to sit, but Spur shook his head. "Let's look at your horses," Spur said. "Can you show me your war pony and tell me how you train him?"

There was a touch of a smile on Wantabe's plain, rugged face. Spur knew he had hit on a favorite topic of the Indian leader.

They walked along the stream, then into a small pasture formed by the brush and trees. In the clearing, Spur saw what he guessed were 200 horses. Wantabe called to one of the young boys who hurried into the pack and came back leading a pony by the mane. It was not a beautiful horse, but it had sharp eyes that picked out Wantabe at once and came directly to him.

The horse stood several hands smaller than the average cavalry mount, had ears that lay back, a slight sway in its back and legs that seemed to go off in strange directions.

Wantabe vaulted onto the animal's back and, without using his hands at all, turned the animal, galloped out 50 yards, turned and came racing back to where Spur stood. Again without touching the mount, he brought it to a prompt halt inches from Spur.

"You trained him?" Spur asked.

Wantabe said he did.

"How many horses do you have?"

Wantabe shrugged. "As leader of the band, I must help the widows and those too old to work enough to feed themselves. Often I give them a pony to trade for food and help with their tepee. I must be generous. Now I have only forty ponies."

Spur nodded, stepped back and looked up at the mounted warriors.

"You captured Penny. She is your prize to do with as you please. I will trade for her. I will give you forty more ponies and horses in trade for Penny and our safe journey back to the ranch."

Wantabe snorted, turned his horse and rode off through the clearing into the brushy area to the south. Spur went to the edge of the stream and sat down. It would take a while as Wantabe battled within himself whether to trade his yellow-haired wife for the remarkable windfall of 40 more horses. Spur could wait.

Chapter Ten

Spur waited all afternoon for Wantabe to ride back to the herd of horses. When he came, he was grim faced and angry, but he held in his emotions, sat down across from Spur, folded his arms and stared hard at the white man.

"*Tosi-tivo* is hard man to deal with. I have decided that I trade for yellow hair if I get a hundred horses."

Spur stared at Wantabe with a level gaze that gave away nothing. Spur knew he had won. Now it came down to how well he could bargain and how many horses would come up the long trail from the ranch.

"A hundred more horses would make Wantabe too rich. You would forget the welfare of your band, strut around like a rich man and soon be beaten for the title of clan chieftain. I can't let that happen to you. We can bring forty-five horses."

Wantabe snorted and threw a rock into the

stream. "Might come down to ninety-five horses if they are all strong, have good legs, can become Indian ponies."

Spur chuckled and shook his head. He knew now that there was some flexibility here. He had no idea where they would end, but he was sure now that they would reach an agreement.

Two hours later they still sat near the horses and the small stream. Twice Wantabe had stood and walked off and seemingly fought with himself over the bargaining.

Just before sunset, they came to an agreement. Sixty horses, 30 now and 30 more when they could be rounded up within two weeks.

They went back to the tepee and ate some small cakes made out of something Spur didn't want to know about. There was rabbit roasted over the open fire, and it was delicious. Spur did wish he had a touch of salt for the meat.

He talked to Penny when the food was gone.

"What did you decide?" she asked, her brown eyes glistening.

"We struck the bargain. You are now the most expensive wife a Comanche has ever traded. Your father will give up sixty horses for your safe return."

Penny squealed in delight, threw herself into his arms and hugged him tightly.

"This is so great!" Penny shouted. "I'll be free again and can do whatever I want to."

"One more thing," Spur said, unwinding her arms from around him. "As of this day, you are no longer Wantabe's wife. He has promised that you are his daughter, and he will care for you and protect you for the next week as his daughter, until I can drive those horses up from the ranch. You must be the perfect daughter as well. Learn all you can from his wives. It may come in handy sometime for you to have firsthand experience with the Comanche."

Spur left that evening as soon as the supper was over. He shook hands with Wantabe, promising that he would return within the week and that no soldiers would come. His cowboys would be wearing their six-guns, but there would be no hostilities of any kind.

Spur jogged downstream, then cut up into the range of small bluffs and brushy slopes to the spot two miles away where he had left his horse. She had been tied near a stream for water and had cropped all of the grass down for as far as she could reach.

He packed up his gear, filled his canteen and saddled the mount in the dark. It would take him two full days of riding to get back to the ranch, but at least he would have good news.

Spur ran out of food the middle of his second day, so he pushed faster to get back to the ranch. He pulled in just before suppertime and rushed to wash up and get to the crew's table. Before Spur had finished eating, the senator came in and waved at Spur.

"Heard you were back. What the hell happened?"

Spur painted the picture for him of the bargaining, leaving out the fight and contests. When he came to the final figure on the horses, he hesitated.

"Come on, McCoy, it can't be that bed. How many horses did you give away to get my little girl back?"

"Sixty."

Delight flooded the senator's face. He nodded and then laughed. "Damn good work! I was figuring he'd demand at least seventy-five. You do good work,

McCoy. I'll tell the president that the next time I talk with him."

Ed Hunt, the Bar-W foreman, had stood close by, listening. Senator Wallington turned to his top rider. "How many nags we got in the corral ready to go?"

"Forty-five, counting them three skinny-looking Indian kind of ponies."

"Wantabe loves those ugly-looking horses that run fast," Spur said. "Let's get them moving first thing in the morning."

"You just came off a two day ride," Senator Wallington said. "You want a day to rest up?"

"Not with Penny up there in that Comanche camp. Something could go wrong to change things up there. Let's move them out in the morning. Probably take us most of three days to drive them that far."

"I'm going," the senator said.

Spur frowned. "How long has it been since you've ridden a horse for five days running?"

Wallington laughed. "Probably twenty years, but I'm going—and no arguments. If I hold up the group any, somebody kick me right in the ass end and get me moving."

The foreman shook his head. "Senator, we might have a problem. Remember that bug I said was going around the crew? We got ten more men down with it. Doc said it was the influenza or some such thing."

"Damn flu?" the senator roared.

"The same. That leaves us about ten healthy hands, and Doc said they could get hit with the flu anytime. Three days riding up and two more back might be something we shouldn't risk right yet."

Senator Wallington looked at Spur, who said, "I've seen the flu kill half a town. Best we be careful of it. Penny is in a good spot up there. I trust Wantabe. He said he'd protect her like a daughter, and she seemed to be getting along fine with the warrior's two wives. Guess I'd have to vote to put off our trip for a couple of days if that will be better for the crew."

"Goddamn," the senator said. "Hell, all right. Two days. If no more of the men get the bug, we'll head up that way then. I want my little girl back where she belongs. Maybe we can get together those fifteen more nags for the trade. Let's try that, Ed. First thing in the morning go find them."

"Any report from Fort Griffith," Spur asked.

The senator snorted. "Damn right there was a report. The commanding officer there, some colonel, said he had no authorization to go this far from his fort to punish any Comanches without some definite raid involved. Said he'd sent a report to General Arnold and he'll evaluate the situation. Hell, by then we'll have the whole thing taken care of ourselves."

Spur had another piece of apple pie, polished off his third cup of coffee, then borrowed a bed in the bunkhouse and slept through three card games, a dice game and two small fights.

The next morning he woke up and asked if there had been any more trouble with the Circle J. The men said there was nothing to worry about. Spur had slept in the end of the bunkhouse as far from the influenza victims as he could get.

He washed up and shaved, then headed for town.

Three hours later, Spur had lunch with the sheriff and the district attorney, Orlando Deeds.

"Of course, it's entirely within the law, Mr. McCoy," Deeds said. "The four men who were on the raid on the Bar-W when the one man was killed could be charged with murder. But this is Texas, McCoy. I could indict them, charge them, arrest them and have a trial, but there isn't a coyote's chance in chicken heaven of getting a jury that would convict any one of those men.

"This is cattle country. The four men work on a ranch, and they were doing a cattleman's thing. Burning down barns has been a favorite way of fighting by farmers and ranchers for as long as Texas has been beside the Rio Grande. No way that I, as the prosecuting district attorney, could sway a jury."

"So we don't charge them?" Spur asked.

"We don't charge them."

They finished the midday meal and wandered outside. The D.A. said he had a ton of work to do and hurried down the street. Spur and Sheriff Ben Johnson headed toward the lawman's office and jail.

"Ben Johnson, you low-down sidewinder of a lying bastard. Never thought I'd find you standing straight up anymore. Hasn't some angry cowboy shot your worthless hide full of lead by now?"

The words came from directly in front of them. A man in his thirties with a full, unkempt beard and angry eyes stood with his feet apart ready to draw.

Sheriff Johnson looked at the man and shook his head. "Son, I don't know who you are. You spend some time in prison?"

"'Deed I did, you yellow bastard hiding behind a badge. Amos Nervine is the name. Colorado, remember. Little town called Benson's Corners. You claimed I shot a teller in a bank robbery."

Ben nodded. "Yes, I remember. Nervine, you did kill that bankteller. The other two tellers and the bank owner testified in court that you killed him. You got off lucky with a ten-year sentence. You out already?"

"Out and living to gun you down. Never would have got onto me if you hadn't been so damn tenacious. Got away clean until you tracked us down in the hills. I been building up a good hate for you for ten years, Ben Johnson."

Ben shrugged. "Lots of men tried to gun me, Nervine. Got so I hated killing all of them. Bodies pile up so much that it makes a man stop and think."

"Shut up, old man, and draw."

"Open your eyes, Nervine. I don't wear a gun, don't carry a hideout. You want to gun me down, you go right ahead. Only then you'll hang for sure. Texas law's a bit tougher than Colorado."

"What the hell you talking about, old man?"

"My partner here. What do you suppose he's gonna be doing while you level in on me? He's the fastest gun I ever seen. Probably drop you soon as you clear leather. Then you won't feel a thing. He seldom misses the heart at this distance."

"No gun? You ain't sided? No hogleg? What kind of a lawman are you, Johnson? You get a gunbelt and a hogleg and you meet me right here in an hour. You don't come out in the street, I'm spreading the word what a yellow bellied cur you are, and you won't be sheriff more than half a day. You get some teeth in that mouth of yours and come out in an hour."

Nervine turned on his heel and walked away from them.

Twenty people had stopped to listen.

"Get your Colt, Ben. Don't let him talk to you that way," one of the merchants said. "Prove to him that you can still outdraw skunks like him."

Ben waved at him and walked on toward his office. Spur stayed beside him. Once inside the office Ben sagged against the wall. He struggled over to his chair and shook his head.

"You heard him, Spur. You know how a town feels about a sheriff who can't pack a gun. You know what they'll do."

"I do. We've both been there. Seems to me there has to be a better way. Let me do some cogitating on it." Spur walked to the window and looked out. He'd seen this happen more than once. Twice the lawman had been fast enough to wound the challenger and ride him out of town. The other time a sheriff had died with a well-placed .44 slug. Spur didn't want that to happen here.

He paced to the empty cells and back to the office. A stray thought hit him, and he nodded, letting it germinate and grow. Why not? Worth a try.

"Ben, does Texas have a law against dueling?"

"I reckon so. Every state in the union does now, and there's a federal law. So what?"

"The way I heard it, that man Nervine just challenged you to a duel. That's a conspiracy to commit a felony. What I want you to do is wear your gunbelt without a gun. I've got a feeling that gunman out there is just a little short when it comes to good eyesight. He didn't realize you didn't have a gun until you told him, remember?"

"So I go out there and he puts a bullet through my chest. What will that prove?"

"It'll never get that far. Believe me it won't. I'll stop it and stash Nervine in your jail; then we'll buy him a ticket into the next town down the line.

"This way it'll look like you are there to face him, and when the whole town recognizes that, you'll be safe here."

"Until the next time. Maybe I should just turn in my badge right now and hightail it to Michigan or Chicago or somewhere that nobody knows me."

"Sure, Ben. Maybe you should just lie down

and die. How long has it been since you've been confronted this way?"

"Been over two years now, come to think of it. Been coming farther and farther apart."

"And this just might be the last time anyone recognizes you. Time's been passing, Ben."

Ben shrugged. "Hell, time and me are best friends. We get along fine." He nodded. "Let's give your plan a try. I'd just as soon go right on being sheriff here for another few years."

At the appointed time, Ben Johnson came out of the sheriff's office and heard a shout from 30 yards down the street.

"By damn, the old-timer is coming out to face me," Nervine called. "Never thought you had the guts left to do it. Let's get on with this."

Ben walked into the street, and Nervine shaded his eyes as he walked up within 20 feet of the sheriff and stopped.

"Just want to make damn sure it's you, Ben. Hate like hell to kill the wrong man. Then I'd just have to come hunting you down." He settled himself, placed his boots a foot apart in the Texas dust and bent his knees just a little. His right hand hovered over the butt of the six-gun resting in leather on his right thigh.

"You ready, old man?" Nervine asked. "Ready or not, the time has come. All you have to do now is die."

"Hold it," Spur McCoy barked from six feet to Nervine's left. "Don't touch that weapon or you're a dead man. Ease off and look over here. You're covered."

Nervine scowled and turned so he could see Spur. "What the hell you doing? This is a private affair."

"Not private, Nervine. I'm United States Secret Service Agent Spur McCoy, and you're under arrest for conspiracy to commit a felony. Dueling is outlawed in Texas. You have challenged this man to a duel, you have appeared prepared to fight a duel, and you have indicated you were about ready to draw and shoot at this man. Therefore you are under arrest for conspiracy to commit a crime. Lift your hands and lace your fingers on top of your head."

Nervine hesitated.

"Ever try to outdraw a weapon pointing at your heart?" Spur asked in a deadly tone.

Nervine shrugged. "Hell, you can't hold me long. No jury is gonna convict me of a chicken-shit charge like this."

"You forget, Nervine, that this is Texas. We do things a bit different here, and we don't like people threatening our lawmen. Now march across the street to the sheriff's office. Make no mistake, I'd just as soon shoot you as put you in jail."

Sheriff Johnson waited for them at the office door. He grinned, lifted Nervine's six-gun from leather and pushed the man into the first cell.

"The charges against you will be filed within an hour, Nervine. I'd guess you'll get a year and a day in the Texas state prison. Opening a new one in Austin, so maybe you'll get in there."

Ben came back from locking Nervine in the cell, fired up the little stove and put on the coffeepot. He eyed Spur. "You say you think I should hang out right here and keep using my deputies for the gunwork. You might be right. If it's two more years before another lowlife recognizes me, I might be ready to retire by that time. Who knows?"

He stoked the fire, then looked at Spur. "Now,

tell me what's going on with that daughter of the senator? You been up to the Indians? Hear tell you was supposed to bargain with the Comanches. What happened up there?"

Chapter Eleven

Spur spent a solitary night in the hotel and the next morning checked out and took his gear with him out to the Bar-W ranch. He found eight men still down with the flu but feeling better. Six riders were out rounding up a few more wild horses to trade with Wantabe.

Spur arrived at the ranch about ten in the morning, and two hours later, just after the cook rang the dinner triangle, a rider came boiling into the home place, his horse sweating and wheezing. He ran to find the foreman, then both hurried up to the kitchen door of the ranch house.

Senator Wallington had just sat down to the noon meal with Spur when the two men stomped inside.

"Senator, we've got trouble," Hunt said. He turned to the man with him. "Shorty, tell them what you told me."

"I been riding our far line the way Ed told me to.

Been up there at the line shack for almost a month now. I usually don't ride the far north section, but I'd seen a bunch of young steers and some brood cows up that direction, so I rode up there this morning to tally up and see what kind of critters we had that far into the boonies.

"Few humps and hollows up that direction, and I just came out of a long low place and was about to ride up to the crest of this little hill, when I heard men yelling ahead somewhere. Now, usually I don't hear another human voice for a couple of months at a time, so I hurried up over the rise. When I saw the rustlers, I backed my nag back down quick to get out of sight.

"Up in front, no more than 300 yards, I saw some cowpokes rounding up our stock. Knew they weren't none of our men. I know all our riders by sight, and none of these matched up. I tied my horse and bellied up to the crest of that little rise and watched them.

"Six men on horseback, and they had what I'd figure to be two hundred head of mixed stock gathered—brood cows, a few calves and a batch of yearling steers. They bunched them up, strung them out and drove them away.

"Damn curious, I figured, so I followed them, hanging back so they couldn't see me if they tried. I followed the dust cloud mostly. Sure enough, they turned east. Ain't nothing east of our land but the Circle J spread. We was to the east of the river already, and it looked like they was heading that herd for the Circle J. I followed them all the rest of the morning, and by then I was dead certain they was far across our range line and into the Circle J. They trailed them straight east, not moving much to the south, so they're still up there, to hell and gone.

"Them bastards done rustled two hundred head of your stock, Senator."

Senator Wallington nodded. "Thanks, Shorty. See that you get something to eat and take a rest. If we need to ride up there, I'll want you to come along and guide us." He nodded at Shorty, who hurried out to the cook shack.

"No doubt about it, Senator. Those Circle J hands rustled that stock. Nobody else would come way up there to rustle two hundred head and then drive them so close to the Circle J operation. They could be seen. It had to be Jordan and his band of thieves."

The senator looked at Spur. "Thought you said we had Jordan scared shitless. He don't seem to be much scared right now. Wonder if he's been stealing cattle up there right along?"

"He was scared when I left him the other day," Spur said. "Maybe he talked to a lawyer in town who said a jury would never convict him or his men of murder in that death. He sure doesn't seem frightened now."

"Senator, don't think we've lost any sizable bunch up there or lower down before this," Hunt said. "Shorty keeps close tabs on his area. He'd know in a minute if he lost even fifty head."

"So, what the hell do we do now?" Senator Wallington asked.

"Senator, it wouldn't be illegal for you to trespass on the Circle J lands and ranges to retrieve your rightful property."

"We rustle back our own stock?" Ed Hunt asked.

"That's about the size of it, Ed," Spur said. "How many men do you have who can ride?"

"We have a crew out after mustangs. I'd guess I can get four men who won't fall off their horses up and out of their bunks."

119

Spur looked at the senator. "Want to ride along, Senator?"

"I think I'll pass on this one. I want to be fresh and ready to go with the horses to bring back Penny."

An hour later they left. Shorty said it was a good three hour ride north to the edge of the Bar-W range, then another three hours east into the Circle J before they'd find the cattle. He told them he wasn't sure that they had stopped them there. But as he left that morning, the dust cloud didn't move any farther east, so he figured the drive had halted.

With Spur, Shorty and Ed Hunt, they had seven men. Each had a rifle on his saddle and a six-gun. Spur wasn't expecting any trouble, but he figured to be ready. If they had six riders to drive the animals, there was a good chance at least two of them had stayed with the herd.

It would take a good day to rebrand 200 head, especially if they had to blank out the Bar-W brand and then brand on the Circle J. There was a chance they would wait for a few days before they branded them. Spur figured that, if he'd engineered the theft of the animals, he'd do the branding as soon as he could heat up an iron.

They cut down the travel time a little by setting their horses into a lope for half the ride.

The group arrived at the boundary line of the Circle J range a little after 3:30. They charged on. Another two hours would make it 5:30 by the time they found the herd.

Spur pushed the horses a little faster. This time of year it would be fully dark by seven o'clock. If there was a moon they could still drive the herd back, but he didn't know how long it would take him to show the law and talk any guards out of the animals.

It turned out to be more than a two-hour ride. It

was after 6:30 when Spur sighted cattle ahead on the rolling lands that dipped but never quite went out of sight.

They saw no horsemen, no line shacks, no smoke. Spur rode with the other men into the herd.

"Damn, mostly Circle J beef here," Hunt said. "There's a Bar-W brand—and there and there. Mixed our animals in with theirs."

Spur stood in his stirrups, then rose up to stand on his saddle so he could see farther. He spotted a lone rider move along a depression no more than 300 yards away.

Spur dropped into his saddle and urged his mount forward.

"Be back," Spur bellowed behind him. He drew the rifle from the boot, levered in a shell and sent a round over the head of the fleeing horseman.

The man turned and stared a moment, then held up his hands, letting his horse slow down to a walk and finally stop.

"Who the hell are you guys?" the Circle J hand demanded as Spur rode up, keeping him under the rifle.

"Who are you?" Spur asked.

"Larson. I ride with the Circle J. This is Mr. Jordan's range."

"Figured that. Where are the other five men who rustled two hundred head of Bar-W beef?"

The man shook his head. "Don't know what you're talking about."

"Didn't think you would. Get off your horse."

The man stepped down.

"Drop your gunbelt on the ground. Now!"

The man scowled, looked at Spur's rifle and dropped the belt and six-gun.

"Now your boots—pull them off," Spur directed.

"My boots? Now see here."

Spur sent a rifle slug slamming into the ground a foot from the man's boots. Larson jumped, sat down and took off his footwear.

"You're doing fine. Now take off your pants and your shirt and put them on your boots.

"See here, I'm just a working ranch hand. You mad at somebody, you see the boss."

Spur fired the Spencer rifle again, the bullet whacking into one of the man's boots and jolting it three feet away. "Your shirt and pants, right now."

The cowhand sighed, took off his shirt and range jeans, then stood there in his long johns.

Spur nodded and waved at the man. "Fine, you're free to go. All you have to do is walk back to the Circle J and tell your boss that the beef he rustled from the Bar-W found their way home again. You also tell him that Secret Service Agent Spur McCoy is going to bring rustling charges against him. As you know, that's a hanging crime in Texas. Now git!"

The man stared at Spur a moment and then began picking his way through the wild range country of west Texas toward the Circle J ranch. Spur gathered up the man's boots and clothes in case he decided to come back and look for them. He'd carry them a couple of miles to the west and discard them.

By the time Spur got back to the herd, Ed Hunt had rounded up what he guessed were 200 head of beef. It was fully dark by then, and they had to work slowly.

"Can't be sure they're all ours," Ed said. "Too dark to see some of the brands. But I'd guess that most of these are ours, so we'll take about two hundred, more or less, to balance the scales."

"Sounds fair," Spur agreed. "You may have some rebranding to do, but I wouldn't worry about that. Fair is fair, and you won't have any problems getting rid of the rebranded stock."

Spur rode around the gathering and tried to count, but it was impossible. Come daylight they could get an accurate count, and if they had too many, they could weed out some Circle J brands and drive them back across the property line.

They drove the unhappy cows and steers and a few calves across the Texas range. The animals thought they should be bedding down somewhere, so progress was slow with a lot of yahooing and slaps of their hats. Now and then a lariat sailed out to rope an animal and drag it along a while until it got the right idea.

It took them five hours to push the cattle over the boundary line and into their own range as far as Ed Hunt thought was safe. By then the men and the animals were all bitching and tired, and Ed told the men to settle down for the rest of the night with their blankets.

At sunrise, Spur came awake and walked through the herd, checking on brands. He figured maybe 70 percent were Bar-W brands, so they wouldn't have a lot to rebrand. The brood cows with the Circle J marks would present no problems, since they would remain on the Bar-W range.

The men rolled out shortly after daybreak and groused about no breakfast. Ed checked the herd once more, and they drove the critters another three miles deeper into Bar-W land. Spur had made a rough count and decided they had about 220 cattle. Close enough for range work.

At Spur's verification of the count, Ed Hunt yelled at the hands, and they all rode for the ranch.

When they got to the Bar-W the cook whipped them up a big late breakfast. The men ate scrambled eggs, country fries, a barrel of coffee, toast and jam and then stacks of flapjacks and bacon.

After the meal, Spur conferred with Senator Wallington.

"I guess both of us should ride over and have a chat with Jordan at the Circle J," Spur said.

"Jordan? That old robber baron? He's been stealing his way into becoming a rich man. I don't want to have anything to do with him."

"I suggest that you come along. Say as much or little as you want to, but if you don't, this thievery and rustling and small sporadic range war is going to continue until it gets to be downright killing time."

The senator, used to compromising in the senate, at last agreed to go.

They got to the Circle J about three that afternoon, and a rifle-toting guard met them at the entrance to the lane. When Spur showed his badge, the rider reluctantly led them up to the back porch.

Ray Jordan was holding a shotgun when they rode up.

"Don't want you on my land," Jordan bellowed.

"Ain't your land, Jordan. You stole most of it, and you're just squatting on the rest like some Missouri mule," Wallington shouted back.

Spur held up his hand. "Enough. I'm here as a lawman of the United States government, Jordan. Last night six of your men rustled two hundred head of cattle from the north range of the Bar-W. I'm here to tell you we have an eyewitness who saw the whole thing and who will help bring charges against you. You know, rustling is a hanging offense in Texas."

"Hell, you can't prove anything. One witness? It's his word against six of my hands. No jury would convict me."

"This isn't a barn burning or a little prank of shooting out windows, Jordan," Spur stabbed back at him, his voice low and deadly. "This is a hanging felony. You and those six men could all stretch hemp, and you damn well know it."

"Not a chance."

"Has the D.A. served you with a warrant against yourself and those four cowboys on that murder?" Spur asked.

"Hell, no. You know he ain't going to. This is cattle country. Them boys was just funnin', and you know that, too. Besides, them four boys decided to draw their pay and move on into Kansas to do their ranch work. Be hard to find them now."

"Rustling is a different charge, Jordan. You've made a lot of enemies in this area. Wouldn't be hard to get a jury who would just be delighted to hang you for rustling. I understand that's how you built your ranch in the first place."

"Smoke and hollering, that's all you've got."

"You'll be able to tell the judge about that. I'm riding on into town now and write up charges against you and those six men for rustling. Sheriff tells me that the circuit court judge will be here day after tomorrow, and his docket is open. We could have a trial going by Friday."

"Now look here, you got no right . . . I can't control all the men I have. How would I know if they decided to drive a few cattle over the boundary line that they thought was ours?"

"In broad daylight with their brands showing? You'll have to do better than that. We'll see you in court, Jordan. I just hope you have a damn good lawyer. You're going to need one. Until you hear from the sheriff with the warrant I suggest that you keep a damn tight rein on your riders and your shooters. The U.S. Government simply won't put up with anymore of your skullduggery. While I'm in this area, I'll damn well see to that."

Spur and the senator hadn't stepped down from their saddles. Now they wheeled their mounts and walked them sedately away from the ranch house. This time Spur didn't feel the itch on his neck and knew that Jordan hadn't trained the shotgun on their backs. He was starting to make progress with Mr. Jordan.

Chapter Twelve

By the time Spur and Senator Wallington rode back to the Bar-W, the crew had returned with the wild mustangs. They had captured 18 of the frisky critters. Some had been strays and saddle broken, while others had never felt a rope or a halter around their necks before.

To keep the horses from stampeding away from them, the cowboys had put the horses into strings with lead lines from one horse to the next. They had six strings of three horses each and found they had little trouble trailing the animals the 20 miles back to the ranch.

Ed Hunt had counted his animals twice at the ranch and now came to Spur with the total.

"Way I figure it, we now have sixty-one horses we can take north. Won't have to do it in two batches."

"How do we move sixty horses up to the Indians?" Spur asked.

"I'd take a page from the mustang men," Hunt said. "They brought them back on lead lines. I'd suggest we put six on a line and use ten men and ride them north."

"Can one man control six mounts on a lead line?" Spur asked.

Ed Hunt pulled off his Stetson and scratched his thinning hair. "Hell, Spur, I don't know. Looks easier than trying to drive that herd north. Say we only have ten wild mustangs who would spook. They'd spook the rest of the herd, and we'd be from now to January rounding them up again."

Spur nodded. "Looks like you have a good idea. Let's try it. Can you dig up ten men for the trip?"

"Yep, long as you and I handle one string each."

They asked the men who would like to play follow the leader, and Ed picked out the eight cowboys he thought could do the job. The senator would not have a string to mind. He led Penny's favorite mount—a little black she helped to raise.

Spur had a good night's sleep in the bunkhouse. The men were quiet, especially the eight who would be riding into a Comanche camp in the next day or two. Did they really want to go? Would any of them come back alive?

Before he went to sleep, Spur talked to the eight and told them that Wantabe was an honorable Indian. "He'll do what he says he will," Spur told them. "He made a bargain with me, and he kept it even when I beat the man he set against me in a test. You'll all come back, and we'll bring Penny with us."

The next morning, they got up with the roosters and crowed back at them, while Ed parcelled out the horses. They made rope halters for some of the animals. Ed made sure that no more than two of the wild mustangs were in any string of eight.

They had a big breakfast, and the senator found he had another horse in his short string. He had the pack animal the cook had loaded up with enough food for the ten men for four days.

"After that you shoot rabbits or rush back here for some of my biscuits and gravy," he shouted at them as they rode off.

Spur led the troop with Ed Hunt beside him. Each had his string of eight horses, and for the first hour all went fine. Then one of the mustangs decided he didn't want to go any farther and set all four feet and skidded Ed's string to a halt.

Ed handed his lead line to Spur, went back to the sullen bay and had a short talk with him, eyeball to eyeball. Then Ed hauled out his six-gun and slammed the barrel down across the horses head just below his eyes.

It was a hard blow. The horse staggered for a moment, went down on one knee, then came upright, ears perked forward. Ed grabbed the bit in the mustang's mouth and led him forward to the rump of the next horse.

"Give them a try, Spur," Ed called out. "Lead away."

Spur kicked his mount into motion and led both strings forward at a walk. Again the bay mustang set his feet and skidded to a stop.

Ed walked up to the horse, caught the bit in his hand and whacked the animal across the bony long head below his eyes. This time the stallion bellowed in anger and went down on both front knees. At once he came up, but this time his eyes were not angry.

"One more time, Spur," Ed called. Spur led the horses out at a stiffer pace this time. Ed yanked on the bay's bridle, and he moved forward on the lead line, letting it go slack but still walking in line. Ed stayed beside the mustang for 100 yards, then ran back to the front of his string and stepped into the saddle.

"Don't think we'll have any more trouble with that bay," Ed said. "I used a little horse sense on the critter and he finally understood me."

They traveled the rest of the day without incident. Just after dark, they found a small stream and settled down around it. All of the mounts were kept on the lead lines, and their front feet wore hobbles.

"No chances any of these are getting away," Ed said. "Otherwise I figure I'll be the one walking back home."

One of the hands had volunteered to be cook. He had two of his friends help him and cooked up some reheated beans, warmed up some biscuits and country-fried a mess of potatoes. It was the two gallons of coffee that at last filled them up.

The next day they didn't make as good a time. Twice they had to stop and straighten out problems with the strings of horses.

They were lined two wide and five deep. It was nearly four o'clock when Spur realized they could never get near the Comanche camp by dark. He found a small stream in the shadows of the Staked Plains bluff, and they started to set up camp.

Without warning a rifle shot ripped into a rider's upper arm, tore through and left him screaming on the ground. Spur yelled for everyone to take cover, and half a dozen more shots jolted into the small low place, but none of the horses were hit.

"Indians," Spur said. For just a moment he wondered if Wantabe had double-crossed him and sent out a large party to attack him and the horses, then claim they never arrived. He doubted it. Wantabe had been straight with him.

They saw two Indians show themselves on the rim of the small hill and then vanish.

"Keep alert. They don't want us; they want the horses. If they don't attack soon, they'll wait for dawn. Most of these Comanches hate to fight at night. They might not even be Comanche. We'll wait them out."

An hour later the sun went down, but there would be at least another hour of twilight.

Spur tried to pick off one Indian who appeared every five minutes and sent a shot near one of the cowboys. All the men were well hidden between horses now.

"They want the horses," Spur told Senator Wallington.

"Damn well ain't going to get them," he said. "These are for my daughter, and nobody is going to get them away from us."

"I figure it isn't a large band or they would have attacked us already," Spur said. "They like the odds in their favor. Might not be more than five or six of them. The trouble is one good rifleman can keep us pinned down in here."

They waited uneasily until darkness; then Spur found Ed Hunt.

"Two or three of you stay alert. I'm going to go out and see how many of them there are and figure what I can do about it."

Ed Hunt grabbed his arm. "Not a good thing to do, Spur."

"I've been around Indians before. If I don't come back, then it's your job to get these horses on up this valley and over the low pass into the next valley to the left. You can't miss it. Wantabe is the man to see. Don't worry. I'm not about to trade in my Stetson for a pair of wings quite yet."

Spur put a sixth round in his revolver and headed out on foot, angling back the way they had come for a hundred yards. Then he worked up the small hill to the right and began to circle the spot where the horses and the nine men lay.

He had gone only 50 feet when he heard something ahead. Two Indians were talking in low tones. Then he saw one get up and jog into the night, moving mostly north, which would be upstream on the small creek.

Spur moved in toward the remaining Indian. He crept forward like a Chiricahua, like the young warrior who had taught him many years ago. Never make a sound. Stay low and close to the ground. Move like a mountain lion through the deep woods, always ready, always alert, always watching.

Spur advanced a dozen feet and froze. The Indian ahead laughed softly to himself. Then he lifted up and fired a rifle down into the area where the horses were. When Spur saw the man stand, he moved swiftly to let the rifle shot cover his sound. When the sharp crack of the shot echoed away, Spur was within six feet of the savage.

Spur had out his knife, as he took soft steps toward the Indian. At the last moment the savage turned, surprise showing on his face in the half moonlight. Spur dove the last three feet at the crouching man, hit him on the shoulders and wrapped his arm around the man's throat. Then he brought up the knife to rest against his chest.

By choking the warrior enough, Spur knew the man couldn't cry for help. The wiry Indian squirmed in Spur's heavy grasp, then seemingly gave up. Spur relaxed for just a second, and the warrior's hand flashed up with a knife aimed at Spur's throat. Spur rammed his blade forward into the Indian's chest. The blade sank in to the hilt, and the thrust of the enemy's knife faltered, then stopped as his hand fell.

Spur heard a long gush of air from collapsed

lungs and knew that the warrior had fought his last battle.

A moment later Spur was on his feet, jogging in the same direction he had seen the other Indian take. It was 300 yards away around a slight bend in the small stream where Spur saw the flickering firelight and smelled the wood smoke. They had camped out, probably planning on rushing the hapless white men in the gully in the morning's first light.

Spur edged up to where he could see. He saw eight men around a campfire eating something they had just roasted.

Two spoke near the fire; the rest turned to blankets rolled out on the ground and went to sleep.

An hour later the last two warriors gave up their talk and lay down on their blankets.

Where were their horses? He hadn't heard any horses on his way here, so they must be the other way. Spur moved around the sleeping camp at a safe distance so they couldn't hear him. It was 200 yards upstream that he found nine horses. It was a nine-man raiding party. Strange size.

Spur watched the horses for half an hour, checking every spot where a guard might be hiding. He found no one. He counted the horses again in the faint light and again saw that there were only nine. There couldn't be a guard, not even a teenage boy, because he would have a horse of his own.

Spur moved up on the mounts cautiously. Any loud noises would awaken the Indians. He approached the animals slowly and gently, making no sudden movement. They were hobbled with leather thongs and picketed on a thin line of leather that any of them could break if so desired.

Spur's plan came full-blown. Steal the Indian's horses. What a great joke on the raiders! How embarrassing! He could just imagine a warrior telling the council how his raiding party had lost nine horses to the hated white man.

Spur checked the ties on the picket line. All the animals were tied to hackamore halters. He cut the hobbles, then freed the line from thick brush and gently led the nine animals on the string away from the Indian camp. He circled around their fire the way he had before, only this time a quarter of a mile out. When he found the stream again, he figured he was well below where the Indians slept.

He tied the horses and found his own men about where he figured they would be.

Now was the hard part. He went from man to man, waking each one up.

"We're moving out. The guard above is gone. I've got all the Indian's ponies. We need to be several miles away from here by daylight."

The men yawned and groaned and bitched, but they got up and readied their strings of animals for a quiet move. Spur went back and brought up the nine Indian ponies. He tied them to the lead line behind the packhorse and whispered to the senator.

"Today you get the honor of stealing nine Comanche ponies from a Comanche raiding party. This will be a real tall tale you can tell your friends in the Senate some cold wintery night in Washington."

They moved out in single file with Spur at the lead, followed by the senator; Ed Hunt brought up the rear. They left the depression along the creek with almost no noise at all and in half an hour were a mile away. Spur kept them moving. He could recognize the terrain in the soft moonlight. They were still a good half-day's ride from Wantabe's camp.

Dawn broke and the men cheered, hoping they could stop for some breakfast. Spur told them not yet; he wanted a better cushion between them and the raiders.

"Those Comanches are horsemen, but without a horse they can still run for six hours without stopping and cover six miles an hour while doing it. They could catch up with us without a lot of trouble."

An hour later from a small rise a mile behind them, Spur heard a rifle fire, then another. The shots landed nowhere near the horse train, but Spur put his mount into a gentle lope and the horses behind them picked up the pace.

It was the last they heard of the eight Indians who lagged somewhere behind them.

They dropped the pace after two more miles. The Indians must have given up, or they were getting too close to the Comanche camp run by Wantabe.

Either way, Spur was glad when they went over the small rise and were on the way to the second valley. There he called a halt for breakfast.

An hour later Spur rousted them out, and they continued the ride to the Comanche camp. All of the horses were used to the lead lines now, and they had no trouble.

Later that afternoon they worked their way down the last little slope and could see the smoke from Wantabe's camp in the distance. They rode faster now, with Spur in the lead.

Fifty yards ahead they came to a wide spot in the small valley, and before Spur could spit, 20 warriors sprinted into the road, each armed with bow and arrow. They stood defiantly glaring at the white men.

Chapter Thirteen

Spur McCoy led the string of horses, so he was out front and close to the Indians. He put up the friend sign with his right hand. A fraction of a second later, Wantabe charged out of the brush on his war pony, a big grin on his face as he surged up to Spur and gave the same friend sign. He had no weapons and reached out and clapped Spur on the shoulder.

The warriors in the middle of the trail lowered their bows and laughed and wailed and screeched in delight at the joke they had played on the white men. They turned and trotted up the trail toward the Comanche camp.

Wantabe motioned to Spur, and the two toured back along the line of horses. When Wantabe saw the large white gelding in the second string of Indian ponies he stopped and stared at the horse.

"*Blanco*," he said. "Where did you get him?" he asked in Spanish.

As they looked at the horse, Spur told Wantabe

about the ambush and how he stole the Indian's horses.

Wantabe laughed so hard Spur thought the Comanche would fall off his war pony. He wept and screeched and wailed in delight. After they had inspected the horses and rode on to the edge of the village, Wantabe tied the ten strings of horses together and waved the cowboys aside. He then paraded the horses through the center of the village, all sixty-nine of them, nodding and waving at the people and shouting now and then at a warrior here and there.

It was obvious that Wantabe was in his glory. He had made the greatest trade of his life, and he wanted everyone to know about it.

At the far side of the village, he gave the string to two young boys, barking orders at them. They hurried the horses into the pasture, quickly untied them and let them roam free in the small contained area.

Wantabe hurried back to the village. He found Spur and the other white men waiting for him outside his tepee. The cowboys stared at the Indians. The Comanche warriors and women alike stared back at the *tosi-tivo*. Spur couldn't see any children anywhere. They had been hustled inside and away from any danger.

Wantabe called sharply at the flap of his tent, and Penny ducked under the buffalo hide and walked out.

Senator Wallington cried out in joy, rushed forward, caught Penny in his arms and hugged her as if she would get away from him.

Penny wore the white doeskin dress Spur had seen before. Her hair had been washed and combed and flowed around her shoulders like a blonde waterfall.

Neither the senator nor his daughter could talk for a moment. They simply clung to each other, and tears of joy rolled down Penny's face.

Spur turned to Wantabe. *"Blanco?"* he asked.

Wantabe chuckled and then roared with laughter again. He wiped his eyes and told Spur in Spanish that *Blanco* was the prized horse of Walking Bird, the leader of the Walking Bird band of Comanches who were camped three long days ride to the north. Walking Bird had boasted what a fine war pony he had and that it could outrun any other horse on the plains. Walking Bird was Wantabe's boyhood friend and his cousin.

Wantabe said for a white man to steal a whole raiding party's horses was a coup that Spur must be proud of and that Walking Bird would never live down.

Spur said the Indian ponies were for Wantabe to do with as he wished, but he suggested that Wantabe give the eight extra ponies to Sitting Squirrel for putting up such a good fight in the knife-and-rawhide battle he had with Spur and to temper any damage that was done to his genitals.

Wantabe frowned for a moment, then nodded. He called Sitting Squirrel out of the crowd and spoke rapidly to him. Sitting Squirrel bellowed in wonder and delight, ran up to Spur and clapped his hand on Spur's shoulder twice as he gave Spur a huge grin. Then he turned and raced toward the horses.

Some of the warriors edged up to look at the cowboy's horses and saddles. Most had never seen a Western saddle, and they were curious. One cowboy mounted with the stirrup and sat in the saddle to show the warriors. They grunted and laughed and shook their heads.

The senator walked over to Spur, still holding Penny's hand.

"Reckon it's about time we get out of here while everyone is still friendly," the senator said.

"I'm so glad that you came back for me," Penny said to Spur. Her round face beamed up at Spur, and he thought he saw a special surge of emotion. He nodded.

"More than happy to help, Miss Wallington. I'd say you're an extremely fortunate young lady."

"Thank you. I'm going to insist that Papa make the president give you a medal and a raise in pay."

Spur chuckled. "The general wouldn't be happy about that at all."

Spur asked Ed Hunt to get his cowboys saddled up. Before they could move Sitting Squirrel shouted from the side of the gathering and came charging through with his own private string of eight Indian ponies that he had just been given. He spotted Spur, jolted his mount to a stop, leaped off and ran up to him.

Spur stood his ground, not quite knowing what to expect. Sitting Squirrel whipped out a fighting knife and charged the last few steps. Spur never moved. Sitting Squirrel stopped a foot in front of Spur, held up the knife and picked up Spur's left hand. He held it up, laid his thumb beside Spur's, then sliced both with the knife. He dropped the knife and pressed his bloody thumb firmly against Spur's bleeding thumb.

He grinned, and Spur laughed and nodded. They clapped each other on the shoulder, and Sitting Squirrel turned, vaulted on his horse and led his string of mounts back toward the pasture, bellowing out a war cry all the way.

Wantabe nodded and looked at Spur. "You know?" he asked in Spanish.

"Blood brothers," Spur said in the same tongue. He turned to the whites. "Sitting Squirrel is delighted with his gift of eight horses. It makes him a wealthy and respected warrior. He just made us blood brothers by mingling our blood. That means that any time we meet, we will gladly give up our lives to protect the other one. A friend for life."

They all mounted. Penny was pleased that her favorite horse had been brought for her ride home. Wantabe walked with Spur as they went to the edge of the village.

He touched Spur's shoulder. "Be careful. Walking Bird might wait for you to return. Go back by a longer route, farther from the Staked Plains. Walking Bird may wait for you to take your scalps and your horses so he won't be ridiculed when he returns to his band."

Spur understood most of the Spanish—Walking Bird, different route, take scalps and horses. He thanked Wantabe. After they clapped each other on the shoulder, Spur mounted and rode off.

As soon as they left the breaks, Spur angled them to the east, away from the towering rim of the Staked Plains bluffs. By the time they came to the area where the Indians had attacked them, they were 15 miles to the east and Spur hoped out of any area where Walking Bird and his Comanches could be lurking.

They made good time the remainder of the day and rode two hours after darkness, hoping to confuse or lose any Indian lookouts who might be watching for them.

Spur put out two guards to the west, then approved a fire to cook the first food they had eaten since their late breakfast. Spur didn't expect any trouble at night. Dawn would be a different matter.

When dawn came Spur rode a circuit around camp, but found no hostiles. They had a big breakfast from a dwindling supply of food. The meal would have to last them until darkness. The threat of the Comanches was still there, but Spur admitted that it was less now.

After the meal, they rode. Spur kicked the pace up to a lope for an hour, then settled them down to a fast walk. Ahead he saw a small depression. He had been heading generally due south now, knowing he'd have to cut back west a little to hit the Bar-W range. He didn't like the looks of the swale. It would be a perfect spot for an ambush with riflemen on both sides.

He had no idea how many of the Walking Bird band had rifles, but he figured two or three. That would be enough on that high ground. He swung to the west, going around the depression but finding himself in a dead flat, probably an old lake. He still had the high ground to the left.

Nothing was perfect. He lifted the mounts to a higher speed and was halfway across when the first rifle shot blasted from the high ground to the left.

The shooters were 300 yards away, effective range for most rifles.

"Turn and ride due west!" Spur yelled at the men and Penny. They all turned and rode to cut down the broadside target and to get out of range.

Spur yelled at Ed Hunt, and they peeled off and rode in a wide circle back the way they had come.

"We'll get behind the ridge and cut off the shooters," Spur called to Ed as they hunkered low on their mounts, leaning a little off the left side to make as small a target as possible.

"They won't want to shoot the horses," Spur called. "A scalp isn't worth as much as a horse to a Comanche."

Soon the firing toward Spur and Hunt stopped,

but they kept shooting at the ten riders getting out of range.

Spur and Ed got to the end of the little ridge that the Indians had used as their shooting gallery.

"They don't have any horses, so they can't move fast," Spur said.

A rifle slug whizzed past Spur, and he dropped off his mount to the side. Ed Hunt bailed out as well.

"Up the slope," Spur said. "I'd guess two of them. I only heard two separate sounds of rifles. Let's work up slowly and flush them out."

They worked upward on the sparsely carpeted ridge. It had some sage, a few bushes and numerous rocks that gave them cover.

They were halfway up when Spur saw movement. An Indian rose up and ran from one rock to another one. Spur stopped, settled down behind his boulder, angled his Spencer rifle at the far edge of the rock where the Indian had taken cover and waited. There were two more rocks about the same size 20 feet away in the direction the warrior had been moving.

Spur waited. Ed saw him and stayed put.

Spur rubbed his eyes, squinted, blinked once, then lifted his brows to keep his eyes open and sharp. Was the Indian going to die there? Patience. Wait him out.

Then a blur showed by the rock, and the Comanche charged away from it toward the next rock. Spur tracked him a moment, led him a foot and fired. The .52 caliber slug hit the charging Comanche in the side, drove through his heart and dumped him dead on the ground between the rocks.

He heard a wail of protest to the left; then three quick rounds blasted at Spur's rock where the puff of white smoke had given away his location.

Spur and Ed waited a moment; then both charged

up the rise toward the next cover. There was no fire. They hit the dirt, waited a moment to catch their breath, then made another dash that took them nearly to the top. They heard one shot, but it came from somewhere on the reverse slope and didn't hit anywhere near them.

"He's running," Spur called. They rushed the last ten yards to the top and far below on the slope saw one Comanche trotting to the north. He turned once and shook his rifle at them, then continued on.

Spur and Ed Hunt let him go. They walked back to their mounts and rode out into the flat of the old lake bed to find the others.

When Spur and Ed came to the rest of their party, they were well out of rifle range.

After Ed told the cowboys about the short battle, they moved on south and slightly to the west to make up for their detour.

Senator Wallington lagged a little behind the others, and Spur dropped back to ride with him.

"You really kill that Comanche back there?" the senator asked.

"I'm afraid so. When somebody tries to kill me, he leaves the chance open to be killed himself. I got in a lucky shot."

"Not what Ed Hunt tells me. Seems you planned it out damned well—and when he moved, you nailed him."

"Happens. How do you find Penny? Has she changed much?"

"I can't really tell. I'd say she has more confidence, more strength now than when she was home in Washington. Of course these are two entirely different situations. You say that Indian must have had his way with her, so she's grown up in another way. Damn, she's not much over eighteen and had to go through that."

"From what I can tell she's taken it in her stride," Spur said. "You're a lucky man. Getting kidnapped and raped that way can just about kill some women."

"I guess that's the change. She does seem older, more experienced, like she knows more about life. Damn, wish her mother were still alive to talk to her."

Later that day, Penny moved up beside Spur at the head of the line.

"I want to thank you again, Spur McCoy. I saw you talking to Papa. Does he know about me and Wantabe?"

"About him raping you?"

"Yes. He came to me eight or ten times."

"Your father knows. He's concerned for you."

"I'll make him understand that I'm fine. Getting poked wasn't all that bad. I had wondered about it. Now I know. Flanroo, Wantabe's second wife, the pregnant one, was like a sister to me. She helped me, gave me this dress, made it bearable for me. And I do know about making love now, so that's one thing I won't have to wonder about like most young girls do."

"But, it's not the sort of thing you spread around or talk about either," Spur said. "In some places, a woman defiled by an Indian is considered an outcast."

"Why? What's different between making love with an Indian and a white man?"

Spur chuckled. "I can't believe we're having this conversation. I can't answer your question. I've never made love to an Indian warrior."

Penny grinned and then giggled. She smiled up at him. "Spur McCoy, I just bet you haven't." She turned her horse and went back to ride beside her father, who was showing some strain from the long trek.

Spur slowed down the line of march. They wouldn't get back to the ranch tonight anyway. They camped near the next water they found even though it was only about four in the afternoon.

Penny washed her face and arms in the cool water and lay on her blanket watching the countryside.

"Soon I'll be back in Washington, and I'll miss all of this. I grew up on the ranch. You'll never get all of the country girl out of me no matter how fancy a Washington dance and dinner party may be."

She had been talking to Spur as he walked past. He paused and watched her. "But you'll be glad to get back to a good hot bath and regular food, I'll bet. Have you had enough squirrel stew to last a while?"

She laughed. "We were lucky when it was squirrel. I swear one time it was skunk we ate. It wasn't too bad, but the hunter who brought back two of them stank for two days."

Spur nodded and went to check the horses.

That evening they ate most of the food they had left, but Ed Hunt said they should be at the ranch well before ten the next day. Then they'd have a late breakfast.

Spur decided they didn't need a guard out that night and settled down when the others did. Penny was nestled up beside her father at one side of the camp, the riders and Spur on the other side.

Spur moved a little away from the others, found a spot and spread out his blanket. It wasn't cold, just a little cool. He woke up sometime in the night with a jolt.

Someone was close by.

"Spur, don't shoot. It's me, Penny."

He saw her then, sitting beside him. She had smoothed his hair or done something or other to awaken him. He sat up and she smiled.

"Just wanted to thank you for coming into that Comanche camp. I figured for sure you were dead. The Comanche really hated how you slipped up on them like an Indian. I knew they planned the knife fight the next day, so I gave up. Right then I thought I'd be a Comanche warrior's wife for the rest of my life."

She paused. "Spur, I owe you so much. I figured I should say thank you the way I know best. I learned how to satisfy a man while I was up there." She reached to his crotch and began to rub, searching for his genitals.

"Penny, no."

"Now don't get all noble, Spur McCoy. Don't I excite you just a little bit?" She caught one of his hands and moved it to her breasts. Her Indian dress was open at the throat, and she pushed his hand in to cover one of her breasts.

"Tell me you don't like that, Spur."

"You know I like it—any man would—but you're the girl I came to rescue. I'm not compounding the problem. Besides, your pa would shoot me dead."

Penny sighed. "I know I can't rape you without making a lot of noise. Maybe when we get back to the ranch." She suddenly straddled him and kissed him hard on the mouth, then pushed him down and humped her hips hard against him. Penny eased away from his lips and slid off him.

"I'll try to work out something later," she said, "when we have more time and a lot of privacy."

Penny grinned and faded away in the semidarkness of the west Texas prairie.

Chapter Fourteen

The tired little band of riders made it to the Bar-W ranch the next morning a little after 9:30. A lookout two miles out had seen them coming and rode back to get the cook busy. When the troop arrived, breakfast was ready, and all dove into it without the benefit of hand washing or grace.

An hour later, Spur had washed up and settled down in the shade of the bunkhouse. He dozed, dropped off to sleep once, roused, lifted his brows, took a long breath and went to sleep again. He figured the senator would be recuperating in bed all day.

Spur was getting some saddle sores himself from all the riding. It had been a different assignment from others he'd had lately. What he needed now was a day of doing nothing; then he could get to the nearest telegraph and let General Halleck know that this case was taken care of.

Felt good, getting Penny back. At first he didn't

think she had a prayer. Wantabe turned out to be a reasonable man, but then again few Comanche warriors would turn down 60 horses in a trade for anything.

He dozed again.

Wild, urgent hoofbeats on the hard Texas ground woke him. He stirred, sat up and saw the horse coming in at a dead run. Something had happened. He waited for the rider to charge into the ranch yard, then swing off his mount near the back door of the kitchen. Ed Hunt ran up from the bunkhouse.

"Harley, what the hell is wrong?" Ed bellowed.

Senator Wallington let the screen door slam behind him as he stepped on to the back porch and stared at the rider.

"Senator, we got some trouble over in the west range near the Circle J."

Spur eased to his feet and ambled up to the trio. He could hear the boy's full-voiced report.

"Found them maybe a mile inside our fence line between the two spreads. There's a three-strand wire fence there we put up few years back. Looked like somebody cut the wire, rode through and just shot down the animals."

"How many again, Harley?" the senator asked.

"Twelve head. Six brood cows, three yearlings and three steers damn near ready for market."

Spur elbowed in beside Ed Hunt.

"Best go out and take a look," Ed said and looked at Spur. "You want to come along? I figure this is about the last straw if'n those shots came from Circle J weapons."

"How long they been dead, Harley?" Spur asked.

"Looks like today sometime. They wasn't warm, but didn't have no bird marks on them. I'd say late this morning."

"Might want to send out a wagon and bring in a

steer to butcher," Spur said. "Meat should still be good. I'd be glad to ride along and track whoever shot them."

"If it was Circle J riders?" the senator asked.

"Then somebody's going to get arrested and taken to jail."

A half hour later Spur let out a small sigh as he stepped into the saddle. He had a different horse at least. The wagon had gone out first, heading for the spot. Spur, Ed Hunt and Harley made up the rest of the team.

They rode out a little over an hour and a half, then came to the bodies. Two men gutted the steer and were getting ready to quarter it so they could load it in the wagon.

Spur checked the animals. Some had been dispatched with handguns, the muzzle placed almost on the back of their heads. Powder burns proved this. Three or four had been shot with rifles from longer range. The dozen bodies were scattered over a 100-foot spread.

Spur got off his mount, walked out 50 yards from the last body and began to walk an arc around the dead beef. He found nothing his first trip. He moved out 20 yards farther and this time picked up the trail of two horses, both shod, coming into the killing site. He worked the area again and five minutes later found the prints of two horses heading away from the dead longhorns.

He whistled, and Ed Hunt and Harley rode over to him, leading his mount.

"Two tracks coming in from the east, and two tracks leading out," Spur said. "Let's see where they go."

The trail was easy across the open country. They angled southeast, then cut due east.

"Heading straight for the Circle J home place,"

Ed said. He eased his six-gun into leather. "You expecting any trouble?"

"Nothing I can't handle. If these tracks go right up to the corral, I'd say Mr. Jordan has some explaining to do."

A half hour later they could see the ranch buildings less than a mile away. Spur looked at his small force and noticed that Harley didn't wear a gunbelt. Just as well.

"Anything happens up here, I hope there won't be any shooting. I don't want you to start any," Spur told Hunt.

Ed grinned. "Damn, I like to hear that. I'm not what you'd call an expert shot. Give me three tries and I can probably hit the ground."

Five minutes later, a rifle round slanted over their heads. A rider came up with the rifle poised.

"Mr. Jordan says no strangers can ride his range," the man said. "You three better turn around and get out of here."

"You going to shoot us down in cold blood?" Spur asked the uneasy guard.

"You just go along now. I got my orders."

Spur kept riding toward him. "Son, you better start shooting if you're going to. Mean you'll have to kill all three of us. You ever killed a man before?"

"Now look, Mr. Jordan said you couldn't come on his land. He means it. It's his right. I got no choice." He fired a round into the ground in front of Spur.

As soon as the round went off Spur kicked his horse in the flanks, and it charged forward, covering the 20 feet before the flustered guard could chamber another round. He reached for his six-gun, but by that time Spur had smashed a right fist into his jaw and slammed him out of the saddle. When the guard looked up, all he could see was the black muzzle of Spur's .45.

"Best if you take your hogleg out and hand it over butt first," Spur said. The young rider shook his head, then stood slowly. The rifle had fallen from his grasp. He eased the Colt out of leather, carefully grasped it by the barrel and handed it to Spur.

"Well, now, that's a lot more neighborly. You pick up your horse's reins and walk in front of us up to the ranch house. Your boss and I are going to have a short talk."

Ray Jordan was halfway to the corral this time when Spur rode in, herding Jordan's guard ahead of him.

"What the bloody hell?" Jordan spouted.

Spur had followed the killers' horseshoe prints right up to the corral gate.

"Jordan, get a horse. We're going to town."

"What the hell you mean?"

"I mean you and I are riding to town to talk to the county sheriff. That means you're under arrest. Do I have to shoot you to make you understand?"

"What's the charge?" Jordan asked, not moving.

"Any number of charges. The barn isn't paid for, the rustling hasn't been answered for, and now we've got a case of grand larceny, destruction of property. Twelve longhorns were shot on the Bar-W. The killers' tracks lead straight to your corral, and I'll testify to that in court as an expert witness. You ready to talk about this with the sheriff, or would you rather that your hands load you in a wagon and drive your body to the undertaker? I'm through fucking around with you, Jordan. Now move or draw. You've got that one decision to make."

Jordan looked around. Three of his hands had come from the bunkhouse. All wore six-guns, but they were out of range. Ed Hunt had picked up the guard's rifle and now held it pointing at the ground a few feet in front of the rancher.

"Goddamn it to hell, McCoy. I don't know what you're talking about. I didn't order no cows shot."

"Your spread. Your responsibility. We're doing this all legal. We ride into town and you can talk to the sheriff and the DA. Maybe they'll just let you pay the bill for the barn and the twelve head of longhorns. Six were brood cows worth at least two hundred a head."

"Goddamn!"

Spur looked at the ranch hand who had been on guard. "You, go saddle up your boss's favorite horse and get him back here in five minutes. Move!"

An hour and a half later, Spur and Ray Jordan pulled up in front of the Sweet Springs sheriff's office. Spur had sent Ed Hunt and Harley back to the Bar-W to tell them what was going on.

Spur got down and waited for Jordan. He groaned and complained about rheumatiz as he stepped up on the boardwalk. Inside Spur found Sheriff Ben Johnson at his desk doing some of what he called infernal paperwork.

"Well, got me some callers," Ben said turning.

"Sheriff, I've arrested this man for malicious destruction of property. I want to swear out a complaint and a warrant for his arrest and have him jailed until he satisfies the charges, or until the circuit court judge arrives to hear the case."

"What happened?" Ben asked.

"This jasper claims I ordered some of the Bar-W stock killed. Somebody shot twelve head, but I swear I don't know nothing about it."

"The shooters came from his ranch on two horses. I tracked them directly back to the ranch's corral. No attempt to hide the trail. A simple case of retaliation for some of the stress this man has been under due to his rustling two hundred head of cattle from the Bar-W less than a week ago."

"Rustling?" Ben said.

"He can't prove a thing."

"This malicious destruction of property is a serious charge," Ben said. He looked at Jordan. "You want me to write up a complaint and get it on the books for the judge? Or do you want to make a statement of charges and keep it unofficial?"

"Ben Johnson, you withered up old son of a bitch! You should know me better than this. I won't pay a damned cent until a court orders me to. What I should do is put a bullet through your withered-up, old, no-good, bony hide."

Ben looked at him with a cold and deadly stare. "You saying you want to try to outdraw me, Ray Jordan?"

"Damn right. You're getting old, Ben. You slowed down. I ain't no gunslinger, but I'm a damn sight faster than an old puny fart like you."

Ben sighed. He reached for his gunbelt and strapped it on, then eased the hogleg in and out of leather. With that checked out, he reached in his shirt pocket, took out a $20 gold piece and dropped it on his desk.

"Well, I figured it'd come to this one of these days, Jordan. You've been running roughshod over your neighbors and half the county—barn burning, rustling, now shooting down steers. Just who the hell do you think you are?"

"I'm Ray Jordan, the man who put the great Ben Johnson in his grave."

Ben tossed the $20 double eagle into the air, caught it and slammed it down on his desk. Heads. "Fine. That's another double eagle for the church. Makes what? Fifty-seven or fifty-eight. I can't keep track. See, Ray, every time I have to kill a man in the line of duty, I pay the church twenty dollars. So far that makes fifty-seven times I've donated. Just wanted to be sure I had the double eagle on my desk so I wouldn't forget to give it to the pastor on Sunday."

Ray frowned. "What the hell is this? You trying to scare me, old man?"

"No brag, just fact. Got it in the records. You can find it under *muerte* for dead. You itching to get into my file?"

"Hell, Ben, that was years ago. You ain't even fired your gun long as I can remember."

"You spend most of your time on that ranch, Jordan. Come on now, I'll get down here at the end of the hall and you stay just about right there. That makes us nigh on to twenty feet apart. About the right range."

Ben walked to the spot and stood there with his feet a foot apart, his right hand hovering over the butt of his old Colt.

"You want to call it or make the first move, Jordan? Don't make no never mind to me. I've killed men plenty of times both ways. Usually the other man's too tied up to be able to talk good."

Ray Jordan stared across the 20 feet at Ben Johnson, one of the best lawmen and fastest guns Texas had ever known. Sweat began to pop out on his forehead.

"From what I hear about you, a six-foot slice of Texas soil out on the far side of the cemetery will be a damn good spot for you, Jordan. Then we won't have no more rustling around here. No more barn burning. No more slaughter of livestock. Yep, I guess it's about time. You ready, cowboy?"

Jordan wiped his forehead and snorted. "You don't scare me at all, old man. Them shootings was years ago. You've gone to seed. I hear you can't hardly hold a fork at the table with that right hand of yours. How you gonna draw and shoot?"

"Way I always have, Jordan. Up to you. I got better things to do than write up another report on a dead body."

"Damn your talk big, Johnson." Jordan took a long breath. "Hell, no sense taking any chances. Maybe I should just pay up the damages and let it go. No sense making a life and death case out of twelve head of steer."

"That and the burned-down barn and shot-out windows," Sheriff Johnson said. "Seems like the rustling came out about even from what McCoy tells me. He give you a figure for the beef?"

Spur, who had backed against the wall, moved up a step. "Figure the six brood cows at twelve hundred, the three three-year-old beef at sixty dollars each, and the three yearlings at thirty each. What does that make, Ben?"

"That's a thousand four hundred and seventy dollars for the livestock. Then there's the barn and the windows. I've got the figures here somewhere."

"It was $2,446 and the windows thirty," Spur said.

Ben grinned "That makes a total of about four thousand dollars. You bring your bank draft with you, Jordan, or shall we go over to the bank for a blank?"

"This is as bad as a Jesse James train robbery," Jordan said, fuming. "Hell, I guess I got to go. Damn his eyes. You tell the senator that he won't see no more trouble out of me. I can't fight the whole damn U.S. government and its secret agents. Goddamn, but I hate this."

"Just stop burning down buildings and shooting cattle and you won't have any trouble with the Bar-W," Spur said. "Oh, and no more dams on the river. That's another federal offense."

"Dam, what dam?" Sheriff Johnson said.

Spur held up his hand. "Nothing that two neighbors can't work out peaceably, right, Jordan?"

The rancher took a long look at Spur, then nodded. "Yeah, something two neighbors can work out. Let's get over to the bank. I make the draft out to Wyman Wallington, right?"

Spur waited for them in the sheriff's office.

Twenty minutes later, the sheriff came back with a bank draft for the whole amount made out to the senator and certified by the bank.

"Well, now, the senator should enjoy seeing this," Spur said, folding the draft and putting it in his shirt pocket. "Looks like I should take another ride out to the senator's place. Oh, we brought back Penny. She's safe and sound and a whole lot wiser. She came through the capture in good shape."

Ben waved Spur back to his chair. "I been thinking. I probably did a damn foolish thing today, taking Jordan up on that shoot-out. Hell, he's no fast draw, but he'd have beaten me by a mile because it would have taken both hands for me to get that damn heavy .44 out of leather. My bluff worked, and I'm damn glad it did.

"Might not work the next time. So I've decided won't be no damn next time. I'm giving my notice today that I'm retiring. Had a letter from my brother in Kansas City. He's got a good detective agency back there. Mostly tame stuff. I can go to work for him, do some office stuff, keep my hand in. Work as much or as little as I want to.

"I'll live in his spare bedroom and not worry about a damn thing. Chances are I'll never run into any of the Wild West bunch I tangled with years ago. I've got a son in Kansas City somewhere. I'll give him a call. Who knows? I might like him. Haven't seen him since my wife kicked me out of the house twenty-four years ago."

He stopped and looked out the window.

"Been a long time." There was another pause, and Ben shook his head. "It's all your fault, McCoy. I never would have decided if you hadn't brought Jordan in here. When I stood over there staring at that man, I knew for certain that he would kill me if he drew. I talked faster than I have in a long time. My draw might be slow, but my damn mouth still works. Right then I figured if I lived another ten minutes, I was going to Kansas City. Be a help to my brother as well. He's ten years younger than I am and a good man."

Spur took Ben's hand and slapped him on the back. "Ben, I'm glad you're going. I didn't know what to suggest. I stumbled around long enough, so you decided on your own. Best advice I've ever given. Now, I better get back to the senator and give him this draft and tell him the good news about Jordan's promise to steer clear of his property. I should be back here to stay the night and get the next stage out toward Abilene. They've got a telegraph there now, don't they?"

Ben nodded and shook Spur's hand again. Spur walked out of the sheriff's office and stepped into his saddle. He should be able to get back to the ranch in time to have supper with the senator.

Chapter Fifteen

Since Penny had come back, the Wallingtons took their meals in the dining room. Spur grinned as he looked over the spread the cook had prepared for them. Penny ran up and kissed him on the cheek, and the Senator beamed.

Penny had spent an hour in a hot bath and now wore a delicious dress that pinched in her waist and showed a hint of cleavage.

"My, what a change from the waif I found in Wantabe's tepee," Spur said. "We have here a beautiful lady."

Penny blushed prettily, and the Senator chuckled.

"She's been my hostess at dinner parties in Washington for two years now and does a great job. Getting better at it all the time. Now I'm going to have to worry about some young blade sweeping in and carrying her off to get married. I've told her she has to complete her schooling first, another year of lower school, then four years in one of the fine women's colleges. I think women should be as educated as possible. They aren't just to be wives and mothers any more. I predict someday we'll have women in the House of Representatives and even the U.S. Senate."

"Oh, Papa, that sounds farfetched."

"Not in the least. I see extremely smart women around Washington all the time. There are women doctors and women lawyers, even women preachers."

Spur had conferred with the senator as soon as he had arrived and given him the bank draft for the damages. The senator had been pleased, especially about Jordan's pledge not to make any more trouble.

"Just hope your friend Ray Jordan makes good on his word about not causing any more problems between our ranches," Senator Wallington said. "Comes right down to it there could come a dry year when we'll have to share the water from the river. Then we'll really need to work together. Below our buildings here the stream bends to the east and cuts across the Circle J land."

"He looked concerned enough to mean it," Spur said. "A nearly four thousand dollar reminder should be enough to keep him in line. Here I think a tough stance helped."

They ate then, a good solid ranch meal of roast beef and four vegetables and rice pudding for dessert.

After the meal, Spur eased back. "I'll be heading into town tonight and then be moving out for Abilene in the morning. I need to find a telegraph so I can tell my boss I'm done with this job and ask for another one. He usually has a stack of them just ready to go."

"No sense in your riding all the way back to town tonight," Penny said. "You should stay here in one of our guest rooms. Those beds at the hotel in town are all lumpy and uncomfortable, I've heard tell."

Senator Wallington agreed. "Absolutely, Spur. You stay here, have a good breakfast in the morning, and you'll still have plenty of time to catch the noon stage out of town."

It was decided.

After supper, Spur and the senator went into his office, where they settled down with long brown cigars and worked at blowing smoke rings at the ceiling. They talked of Washington politics, and Spur told the senator he'd been an aide to New York Senator Harvey Bilbrae.

"That was before I went to the Senate," Wallington said, "but I've heard of him."

"He was a family friend. I learned a lot those two years in Washington."

The senator brought out a chessboard, and they started a game. It had been years since Spur had played, and his game was rusty as a pitchfork in a salt lick. He lost the first game quickly, got his mind working and then played the next game to a stalemate.

Penny came in twice during the games, but went out each time, looking a little unhappy. She came back when she heard they had stopped the last game.

"Time for some regular talk and not a silly old game," she said as they went into the living room. It was the first time Spur had seen it and he was surprised how well it was furnished. It looked like any fancy Washington town house in the best part of the city.

They talked of politics and about the president

and how quickly the western territories were becoming states.

"We're going to fill in this great country from one coast to the other," the senator said. "One day we'll have the whole place civilized with towns and roads and all sorts of modern conveniences we haven't even thought of yet. I'd love to stay just the age I am now and return to the United States say in nineteen hundred and seventy-five, a hundred years from now. The things I'd be able to see!"

Spur agreed, and they then played a guessing game, trying to figure out which territory would be settled quickly enough to become the next state.

"I'm betting on Colorado," Senator Wallington said. "We've had delegations from there for the past two years. They are progressing remarkably well. The gold and silver strikes have helped, of course. That's my prediction."

Spur caught himself yawning and apologized. Then he stood up. "Folks, I'm not good company anymore. I think I better take advantage of that soft bed you mentioned. It's been interesting talking with you both tonight, but I better turn in."

The senator nodded. "I could use a good night's sleep myself. I haven't recovered from that five-day ride. Not used to a saddle anymore."

"I'll show you to your room, Spur McCoy," Penny said. "In Washington we have a maid, but here I get to do most of the housekeeping."

She led the way up the steps, and when they were out of sight of her father, she stopped Spur, reached up and kissed his lips.

"I've been wanting to do that ever since you came back from town."

Spur caught her by the shoulders and moved her back a step.

"Hey, easy. Your father might come up the steps anytime."

"No, his bedroom is on the first floor. We set it up down there so he wouldn't have to go up and down the steps." She linked her arm with his and walked him down the hall.

"You have the best guest room with a big feather-bed and a fine set of springs. I'll turn down the covers for you."

She hurried into the room ahead of him, pulled back a bedspread and fluffed the pillow. When Penny turned around she had unbuttoned the top of her dress so the sides of both her full breasts showed.

"Now, Spur McCoy, a little sample of what comes with the bed. I'll be back after I'm sure Papa is asleep. Once he goes to sleep a cannon shot wouldn't wake him up."

She caught his hand and pushed it over one of her breasts, and when she stretched up and kissed him again, he felt her tongue push hard against his lips.

Spur pushed her back, holding her shoulder with his free hand.

"Penny, this isn't right. I'm your father's friend. I can't do this to him. He'd have me shot before sunrise. You just control yourself a little here. I know you had a rough introduction to making love, but you don't have to try to keep doing it all the time."

She pouted. "I thought you liked me. Your hand feels so good on my titties." She tried to kiss him again.

"No, Penny, you're much too young for me."

"I'm eighteen. I'm a woman now. Lots of girls I know are married and have babies by the time they're eighteen."

"But not you, Penny. You're the daughter of the U.S. Senator from Texas. Someday you'll find a fine young man as talented and educated as you are and you'll marry and be deliriously happy."

She put her hand down and rubbed his crotch. "I just want to be deliciously happy right now, with me flat on my back and you over me and pushing your big poker inside me just ever so many times."

Spur smiled and walked her to the door. "I see the door has an inside lock on it, Penny. You'd make much too much noise if you pounded on it, so you just forget about making love. I'll kiss you once more; then you tell your father good night and slip into your bed all by yourself and be good.

"Oh, damn. I've been good all my life. Now that I've found out about sex and making love, I want to try it again. It would be a great comparison to see if making love with an Indian is different from making love with a white man."

Spur laughed softly, edged her out the door and then gently closed it with her on the outside.

"Good night, sweet Penny. You have pleasant dreams. I'll see you in the morning for breakfast."

Spur settled down on the bed and found that Penny had been right. It was a wonderful bed for sleeping. He thought about the bright young girl a moment; then the busy day caught up with him and he closed his eyes. A minute later he slept.

Spur awoke when the roosters outside in the yard greeted the dawn just past six o'clock. He rose, dressed, put all his gear in his carpetbag and carried it downstairs. The senator was up and reading some papers he had brought from Washington.

"Morning, Spur. I'll be heading back to Washington at the end of the week. I best be read up on this new bill or I won't know how to vote."

They had coffee and breakfast and were just

through when a sleepy-eyed Penny came into the kitchen.

"Morning to both of you, I guess. I'm more of a night person," Penny said. "I detest getting up early in the morning."

Her hair was not combed out and her face still sleepy. She mumbled something, waved a good-bye to Spur and took a cup of coffee back to her room.

Spur had another helping of hot cakes and sausage patties, then shook hands with the senator and headed for the corral. Ed Hunt had pulled out a mount and was in the process of saddling her.

"Just leave this mare at the livery stable," Ed said. "We'll pick her up next time we're in town."

Spur shook hands with Ed, then stepped into the saddle while Ed tied down the carpetbag on the back. Spur took one last look at the ranch, then turned and angled his mount down the lane toward the road that followed the river a quarter of a mile away.

He rode past a line of greenery near the stream where a half-dozen trees from the seepage from the main channel. There weren't enough rivers in Texas, Spur decided. What a wonderland it would be if it just had enough water, laced with streams the way Ohio or Illinois was.

He had almost ridden past the trees when he heard a cry of pain. He stopped and looked at the wooded area and saw a horse under the branches. To his surprise he saw someone lying on the ground near the animal. Again the cry of pain came.

Spur galloped over, dropped out of the saddle and hurried to the person on the ground.

The second he knelt down beside the body, it came alive and sat up. It was Penny.

"Hi, Spur McCoy. You didn't think I was going to let you get away so easily, did you?"

She shrugged out of her already unbuttoned blouse, revealing her bare breasts, full and ripe and with soft pink areolas and deep red nipples that were standing tall and pulsating with hot blood.

"Penny . . ."

"No talk. I'm here and you're here and Papa thinks I'm out riding along the creek to the north. Nobody will ever know, and I want you so bad I'll die if you don't make love to me right here and right now."

She reached up, kissed him and pulled him down on the soft grassy spot. Her tongue worked against his mouth, and he opened his lips and let her explore.

His hand came up and found one of her breasts, and she moaned softly. "Yes, yes, Spur, this is more like what I dreamed about. Now I want you to seduce me slowly and tenderly, like I'm a bride. Will you do that?"

She kissed him again, nibbling around his mouth, then sucking on his top lip until he growled in sudden desire, pushing her slowly back to the grass. He kissed her again, feeling the heat radiate from her whole body. She rolled him over until she was on top, then fed one hanging, throbbing breast into his mouth. Spur sucked and chewed on it until she whimpered and then he bit the delicate nipple.

She screeched in wonder and pushed the other breast into his mouth for its turn.

A moment later she moved off him, sat up and pulled down her skirt. There was nothing under it but her slender, firm young body. He marveled at the beauty of her youth and her sleek body and the way she gently parted her thighs.

She pulled at the buttons on his fly until they came open; then her hand thrust inside to find him. Penny gave a little cry of joy and wonder as her fingers closed around his erection.

"Such a wonderful, marvelous organ," she whispered. Penny looked around and laughed. "I don't need to whisper. I can say out loud that I want you to fuck me. I can tell you to poke me right now, Spur, before I die. Don't take your clothes off. Just push your big whanger into me as far as he'll go. I know I'll die right here and now if you don't push him inside me."

She worked his erection out from his pants.

"Oh, my, much bigger and longer than Wantabe's was. Push it in me, Spur, now!"

She moved on her back, lifted her knees and spread her legs, holding out her arms to him.

A moment later Spur slanted into her, and she gave a great whoop and scream, then settled down and pumped against him with every stroke.

He reached between their bodies, found her small hard node and stroked it four times. Penny looked at him with surprise, then awe, and a moment later her face cringed with pain and wonder as the spasms shook her slender body. The vibrations rattled through her body, making her cry out with a plaintive wail that was half delight and half marvel that such a thing could be happening to her.

Five times she stopped, then tore into another climax as the emotion drilled through her time after time.

Only when it was over and she gasped in amazement did she have the breath to whisper.

"What in the world did you do to me, Spur McCoy?"

"That was your climax. That's what you should do every time you make love, whether a finger has to do it or not."

"There's more than just the poking?"

"Sometimes the climax for you will be from inside,

sometimes outside like now. Both are marvelous and wonderful."

"What about you?" She squeezed him with her internal muscles then, and he was sure no one had taught her how to do that. It was instinctive, as natural as eating and sleeping. He came in a rush, and she squealed in delight as he shot his load deep within her.

He rested with her there on the grass and she looked up, her face so beautiful that he wanted to take her with him on his trips and make love to her every night and morning.

They came apart and rested side by side until she pushed up on one elbow and watched him.

"Better," she said.

"What?"

"It was much better with you than with Wantabe. A whole lot better, I can tell you that." She sat up, and her wonderful young breasts bounced and rolled. "Again," she said. "Let's to it again."

Spur laughed and told her he needed a few minutes to rest and recuperate before he could poke her another time."

"Oh," she said, "I'm learning more and more."

Spur considered the time. Once was never enough for him. The stage didn't leave until noon. He had ridden away from the ranch at a little after 7:30. There was plenty of time.

He lay there staring up at the sky and the trees, listening to the water gurgling along on its way downhill. He felt totally relaxed and at peace.

She kissed him.

"Now?" she asked.

Spur kissed her lightly. "Three or four more times, sweet Penny. Just give me a little more time."

He was thinking ahead. Soon he'd be on the stage moving to Abilene, and there he could send a wire to the general reporting Penny's release and asking for a new assignment. He had nothing on his own personal list that had to be done quickly. The general would have something.

Spur sighed and watched the small puffy clouds. It was a good day to be alive.